MW01659509

Tales From Infirmary Road

by Jessie Moinuddin

Henchard Press, Ltd

Publisher	Henry S. Beers
Associate Publisher	Richard J. Hutto
Associate Publisher	Rick L. Nolte
Executive Vice President	Robert G. Aldrich
Operations Manager	Gary G. Pulliam
Editor-in-Chief	Joni Woolf
Designer	Audra George
Distribution	Nick Malloy

© 2008 Jessie Moinuddin

All rights reserved. No part of this book may be reproduced in any form or by any means without prior written permission from the publisher, except for brief quotations used in reviews written specifically for inclusion in a magazine, newspaper, or broadcast media.

Disclaimer: Henchard Press, Ltd does not assume any legal liability or responsibility for the accuracy of any information or content in this publication. The statements, views, and opinions presented in this book are those of the author, based on her own research and open public records, and do not reflect the opinions or views of Henchard Press, Ltd, its staff, or associates.

Printed in the USA.

Library of Congress Control Number: 2007934435

ISBN: (13 digit) 978-1-934144-20-6
(10 digit) 1-934144-20-7

Henchard Press books are available at quantity discounts with bulk purchase for educational, business, or sales promotional use. For information, please write to:
Henchard Press Ltd., SunTrust Bank Building, 435 Second Street,
Suite 320, Macon, GA 31201, or call 866-311-9578.

The towns of Ridgefield and Foxton and the county of Upshaw, Ohio, and the Upshaw County Home, are fictitious; all of their inhabitants, as well as the characters from Cleveland, and their situations are products of the author's imagination or are used fictionally and are not intended to portray real people or real situations.

DEDICATION

In memory of all County Home/County Infirmary/County Poor Farm residents of the past, especially those—my muses for the writing of this book—whose lives touched and enriched my life.

TABLE OF CONTENTS

ACKNOWLEDGMENTS

I thank Gale VandeBerg, who kindly shared his memories and knowledge of steam threshing operations.

My thanks also go to Judith Ortiz Cofer, Judson Mitcham, and Seaborn Jones for their early encouragement in the writing of some of these stories, and to leaders and members (they are too numerous to mention all of their names) of several writing groups and workshops for suggestions throughout the writing process. I thank also Gail Galloway Adams and Kellie Wells for critiquing two of the stories in progress at a workshop at Georgia College & State University.

I thank especially Pat Landreth Keller for suggestions and sustained encouragement and for reading the entire manuscript at a middle stage of its development.

PROLOGUE

I went to Korea and did two tours in Nam, but the war I *really* ached to get into, World War II, I missed by just a couple of months—I was seventeen, but my parents wouldn't sign for me to join up. Still, the last five *months* of that war, what I did and learned and the people I met, I wouldn't trade for any five *years* of my life since then.

At the time, I wrote down for my high school senior thesis some of what I did as a green city kid learning to be a farmhand at a rural home for old folks and other unfortunates of the county. When I look at that old thesis now, I see it's pretty mechanical and technical—all farm machinery, crops, and livestock. The people are almost invisible. But now, as an old man thinking back to those five months, what I remember most of all *are* the people. And the stories.

A most unretro sort of nostalgia has caught hold of my mind: the stories seem to me so "now" that often I find myself telling them as if they're happening today. I don't think people have changed very much; most of those stories could happen—are happening—today. But seldom in the setting of the poor farm, county infirmary, rural county home, for that venerable institution is fast passing from the American scene.

Will Miller
January 23, 2008

PART ONE

ROAD TO RICHES

At the sign, Infirmary Road, my father turns the Oldsmobile off the paved highway. We're well south of Cleveland, heading toward the Upshaw County Home in that rural area where Dad grew up. Before the name was changed to County Home, the place was called the infirmary, and before that just "the poor farm." The Infirmary name stuck for the road that leads to it. Right now that road is taking me, a city boy, to my first job out of high school—as a farmhand at the home.

Dad is saying, for the seventeenth time it seems to me, "You know, Will, I think you're making a huge mistake, leaving school to take this hick job on the poor farm."

"But Dad, I'm seventeen now, and you and Mom won't sign for me to join the army. I want to do something for the war effort, and I don't think I could stand to work inside in a factory."

"You bet we won't sign! Your cousin Daniel's dead already in the Battle of the Bulge, and him barely nineteen. They'll get you soon enough in the draft. But maybe we'll finish it before then, that's what I'm hoping, so you won't have to go at all."

We've had this talk before. As well as the one in which Dad tells me how he had to drop out of high school and work as a farmhand to support his mother and younger brothers, and how he escaped to Cleveland as soon as he could, took a business course in night school, and worked his way up in the company to sales manager.

"I didn't do all that to have a son of mine going backwards, starting at the bottom as a hand in the same hick county I got out of. You could have finished high school; I had no choice but to drop out."

"But Dad, it's only two months till commencement, and I am going to graduate with my class come June, you'll see. I have nearly enough credits, and the school's going to give me what I lack in English when I turn in my senior thesis about my farm experience. Anyway, they're letting the guys who joined up early graduate, without their finishing the last few months of the senior year."

End of conversation. It could have gone on, with Dad telling me again how I don't know how hard the work on a farm can be, and how I'll be so tired at the end of the day that I won't have the energy to write a word, let alone a thirty-page paper.

We're passing the first of the County Home's gently rolling fields—one showing the new green of winter wheat, one partly plowed, and another a pasture where the home's dairy herd has been turned out. It's an unseasonably warm Sunday in early April, so we have the front windows part way open. Suddenly, Dad rolls his window down the rest of the way and sticks his head out. He takes a deep breath. A trace of a smile flickers over his face. What's this? He really likes the country smell, the rural scene? A bit of nostalgia for this county and the way of life he says he hates? Now I'm smiling at him.

"Dad?"

"What, Will?"

"Thanks for finding this place for me to work."

"You're welcome, I guess. You know, I wonder if I'm imposing on Cousin Abel, foisting a green city kid like you on him. But I feel better knowing it's him who'll be making you toe the line and turn out a real day's work, every day. I went out on a limb for you, getting you this job. Now don't you let me down!"

"I won't, Dad."

"Humph!"

We top a rise in the road. Spread out before us are the home's main building, the gleaming white barns and smaller outbuildings, the lawn, garden, and orchard.

"There's the Hof!" Dad cries out, and now a really big smile spreads over his face. He's been here before. "Just like I remember it!"

"The Hof, Dad? What's that?"

"Oh, that's an old German word. When I was a boy, some of the old Pennsylvania Dutch around here still used it for a place like this, a main house with the outbuildings and the farmlands spread out around it. You probably won't hear it these days. Now most everybody speaks English, except the Amish."

I figure Dad's back on his nostalgia trip again. He stops the car on Infirmary Road in front of the home's main red brick building. The building has three tall stories over a basement in the center, with two-story wings straight out on either side. Each wing has a large verandah. Old men in dark work clothes—blue denim or gray or brown—are rocking and smoking on the right wing's verandah. Other old men are walking up from the barns or sitting around outside on benches, smoking their pipes. In rocking chairs on the left wing's verandah are mostly old women, in cotton house dresses, cotton stockings, and wool sweaters or shawls. There are a few younger women dressed the same way. There's no one in what I would call Sunday clothes, and no one who looks like a visitor.

Dad takes it all in. "I don't know if we should go to the front door of the staff quarters—that's the door in the center section."

He decides against that, starts up the car again, and circles around to the back. There we see a strange-looking little man dozing on a bench. Dad says, "I wonder if that's Cousin Henry. I haven't seen him since we were children!"

I'm thinking to myself, "Good Lord, please let that not be our cousin Henry!"

"Yep, that's him, all right—looks about the same, only older. His hair's gotten gray like mine."

Henry's straw hat has fallen off, disclosing his small head, slant eyes, and stuck-out ears. His tongue is sticking out too. He's a man, not a boy, but he has no hair on his deeply creased face. His arms and legs are too short for the rest of him.

Dad says, "His mama told everyone he got dropped on his head when he was a baby, to account for him lookin' that way and bein' none too bright. But that's a myth. Your grandma saw him when he was newborn, and she knew there was something wrong with that baby right from the start.

"Well, come on, Will. Let's go in and have you meet Cousin Abel and his wife, Nellie. They're officially the superintendent and matron of the home, but you'll call them "Boss" and "Missus," same as everybody does around here. Don't you go calling them "Cousin" or let on they are, lest folks here think you've got some kind of special privilege, bein' kin."

"O.K., Dad."

We go up the back porch steps, cross the porch, and step into the big kitchen, where two women and a young girl in house dresses and kitchen aprons are setting out cold dishes of leftovers on a long table. One of the women has a large ring of keys pinned to her dress. She smiles. "You must be Frank and his boy, Will. We've been expectin' you. I'm Nellie. This is our staff cook, Mrs. Meyers, but everyone just calls her Cook, and this is my daughter, Joy. Now come on up front to the parlor and meet Abel and Ray."

Nellie (I mean "Missus") leads the way. We pass through a large hallway which divides to circle around the broad central staircase. On either side of the hallway I notice closed doors, evidently leading to the men's and women's wings of the building. There's also a carved mahogany gun cabinet; through its curved, heavy glass door I glimpse a shotgun, an old musket, and several pistols.

The small front parlor is not at all formal looking as I had expected something called a parlor to be. Instead, it appears to be an everyday living room for Boss's family and the staff. Boss and Ray are reading the Sunday paper. Boss gets up as we enter, shakes hands with Dad and me, and introduces Ray to us. Ray is a wiry, middle-aged hired hand who doesn't say anything, just nods to us; I feel his eyes taking me in, sizing me up. I guess he doesn't much like what he sees—gangly, skinny, city boy that I am.

Missus says to Dad, "We're fixin' to have a light supper in a few minutes. You'll stay, of course?"

"No. Thank you anyway. I've got to get started back. It takes quite awhile going only 35, you know, and Will's mama will start worrying as soon as it starts to get dark. So I'll say goodbye now."

Dad looks at me as if to say again that I should work hard and not let him down, but he doesn't say it. He just says, "O.K., Will, your mama and I will be seeing you at home in two weeks, when you have your Sunday off. You know how to catch the Greyhound into the Cleveland station and come out to the house by streetcar?"

"Yes. And Dad, thanks for bringing me down here today. I know it used up quite a bit of your gas ration."

As we walk to the back, Boss and Ray lag a bit behind us, and I overhear Ray say, "He's jest a boy—no muscle on him. Can he hack it here as the second hand?"

Boss answers, "I think so, if he's anything like his dad. Anyway, he's all I could get fer now."

Dad leaves for the city. The rest of us light into the "light" Sunday supper—a marvelous array of country dishes, some of which I've never eaten before. I don't know what the next day or the next few months will be like for me here, but my guess is: very different from my life in Cleveland. Like my first taste of headcheese this evening at supper, different, but not bad. Not bad at all.

MILKING AND FITTING

I'm startled awake and jump from bed as a bell clangs not four feet outside my bedroom window. Looking out, I see, mounted on top of a telephone pole, a large bell like that on a steam locomotive. Down below, an old man is pulling the bell rope, again and again. It seems he will never stop. I'm a heavy sleeper, but there's no way I could sleep through that noise!

My room is one of six small narrow staff bedrooms on the back side of the second floor. Three of the other rooms are occupied by Ray, by Cook (Mrs. Meyers) and (I had been told) by Cora, the young woman who cleans the wards. I have yet to meet Cora, as she had not come in from her Sunday off in time for supper last night. Two of the small rooms are not occupied just now. One of these is being saved for Alex, the son of Boss and Missus, who is away soldiering in Europe, while the other is for the downstairs cook when she lives in. However, I was told that the current "downstairs" cook, that is, the one who supervises the cooking of the inmates' meals in the big basement kitchen, commutes to the home daily from her own homeplace a few miles away. I haven't met her either. The front half of the second floor, around past the stairwell, has the bathroom, a sewing room, and the bedrooms of Boss and Missus and their daughter Joy.

I pull on my jeans, socks, and shoes, and head to the bathroom. Ray, freshly shaven, is just coming out of there. I don't see how he could shave so fast.

"Hurry up, there, Boy. We need to get down to the barn for morning chores right away."

I need to shave my chin sprouts only about twice a week anyway, so I decide to do that evenings since mornings seem to be so hurried. I get back to my room and into my shirt as fast as I can, and I grab my work jacket and cap and join Ray. We're downstairs fast and through the kitchen with only a quick nod and a "mornin'" to Cook and Missus. As we go on out through the screened porch and head toward the dairy barn, I notice how the weather has changed from the warmth of yesterday. There is a cold, damp feel to the air, and a fine drizzle begins. There is no trace of dawn yet; the war-ordered daylight saving time is not friendly to the farmer. However, atop a tall pole is a big incandescent electric light which lights the area around the barn and across Infirmary Road.

Ray strides fast toward the barn. I have long legs and easily match the length of his stride, but I'm not used to moving so fast the first thing on getting up, so I have to force up the pace of my steps to keep up with him.

The milk cows are coming out the gate of the near pasture and crossing Infirmary Road. Although several of the able-bodied old men are standing in the road waving their arms, apparently at work directing the cows, the cows themselves move quickly across the road. They must know where their concentrated feed is and where they can get relief from the pressure in their swollen udders; they hurry into the barn. Each cow finds her own stanchion, sticks her head through it and starts eating the feed in front of her.

"Boy, yuh ever milk a cow?" Ray asks me.

"No. I've seen it done but never did try my hand at it."

"Well, here's one 'at milks easy and oughta be good fer yuh to learn on. I'll show yuh on her and then yuh can try it. First I gotta clean off her bag. She's been laying down and got mud caked all over it."

Ray wipes her udder clean and sits down on a little stool. Milk is already dripping from her teats.

"Yuh grab the two front teats, one in each hand, so. And don't spit on yer hands to milk the way some of these dirty old guys do. I can't seem to cure them; they've been doing it that way too long, but I can start you out right."

Ray puts a bucket on the floor and steadies it between his lower legs. He shows me how to squeeze one teat from right up next the udder to the end, then the other teat, directing the streams of milk into the pail. Then he lets me try it.

"When yuh finish the front teats, go on and do the same with the two hind ones."

I feel awkward but I do it anyway. Ray checks that I have got as much out as can be gotten that way. He shows me how to strip the last milk out and I do that too. He peers into the bucket. "That looks about the right amount of milk fer her to give." Ray says that sort of gruffly, but I take it to mean I did O.K. for my first try at milking. He has me add the milk to milk in another bucket. One of the men whose job is carrying now carries that bucket and another filled one up toward the big house.

Ray assigns a second cow to me and I milk her too. Again Ray checks my work. I guess he's satisfied, for he says, "Yuh'll milk those two every time from now on."

"O.K., Ray."

Everyone else in the milking crew has finished, although most have milked four cows while I did my two. The men are already opening the stanchions and letting the cows out.

I peer closely at "my" two cows. Both are Holsteins (I know that much)—the black-and-white-patterned breed. They look quite a lot like each other and also a lot like many of the other cows. How can I remember which are my cows to milk? I try to find something distinctive about each but don't succeed. Just in time, before they are let out, I hit on counting down the rows of stanchions. My first assigned cow is in no. 8 from the east end of the first row, and my second is in no. 10 from the east end of the facing row. That will have to do for now, until I can learn to tell them on sight. I sure don't want to be embarrassed by sitting down at the wrong cow!

The men go on getting the cows turned out and back over to the near pasture. The carriers carry the last of the milk up to the big house. I wonder why they don't just take it to the milk house, which is right next to the barn. But Ray explains that they don't ship any milk; all of it is used right on the farm for drinking, cooking, cream or butter, and since they have a big walk-in cooler at the house for chilling and storing, it would just be extra work to make two transfers when one will do.

***

As we walk up toward the house, that big bell on top of the pole by my window rings out, calling us in to breakfast. We hurry in to the downstairs washroom. Ray hangs his jacket on a peg and motions to another peg where I hang my jacket and cap. Then he rolls up his sleeves above the elbow and runs water into an enameled washbasin that's sitting in a long, galvanized metal trough. He points to another basin. "Yuh can wash up in that one, Boy."

I don't think my arms are dirty; after all, I've had my sleeves down and a jacket over my shirt, but I copy Ray the way he rolls up his sleeves and washes—hands, arms, face and neck—the way a man washes when he comes in from work. There's plenty of hot running water, soap, and a scrub brush for cleaning away grime. To one side a long huck towel is looped over a wooden roller; you roll down a clean part to dry on. On a shelf above the trough is one small comb. Ray grabs it and runs it through his hair. After he lays it down, I pick up it up and copy him, though I can hear my mother's voice saying, "Never use another person's comb!" Her rules don't seem to apply here, or at least I can't apply them without seeming out of place.

We go into the dining room where the table is set and the rest of the staff members are taking their regular places. Cook comes in with a steaming tureen and puts it on the table. As she takes her place at the head of the table, she motions to me where I should sit.

Missus says, "Cora, Will, you two haven't met yet. Cora, this is Will, the new hand. Will, Cora cleans the wards. She helps with other work around here, too." We nod to each other. Cora is about twenty-five, I judge, from her fine young skin and all dark hair. But with round, wire-rimmed glasses, no makeup, and her hair pulled back in a bun, her overall appearance is rather like that of an old lady.

The other new face at the table (new to me, that is) belongs to the inmates' cook, Mrs. Clark. Her deeply wrinkled face and snow-white hair make her appear old enough to be one of the inmates. But she has a nervous energy about her that belies her age. We are introduced too. I soon learn that she eats quickly, says little, and excuses herself early because she needs to get back to supervising her crew of inmate cooks; they are preparing the inmates' meal while we eat ours.

The breakfast is dried beef gravy on toast. I'm surprised, for that is a main dish we would have for supper at home, never for breakfast. Cook says she always serves that breakfast on Mondays, the big wash day, as it is the easiest thing for her to fix. The toast is big thick pieces from bread baked right here at the County Home. It's different from the store-boughten white bread I'm used to.

***

After our staff's breakfast, and while the inmates are having their breakfast, Ray and I go down in the basement to a room just outside the walk-in cooler. There we separate cream from milk. When we finish, we put the skim milk

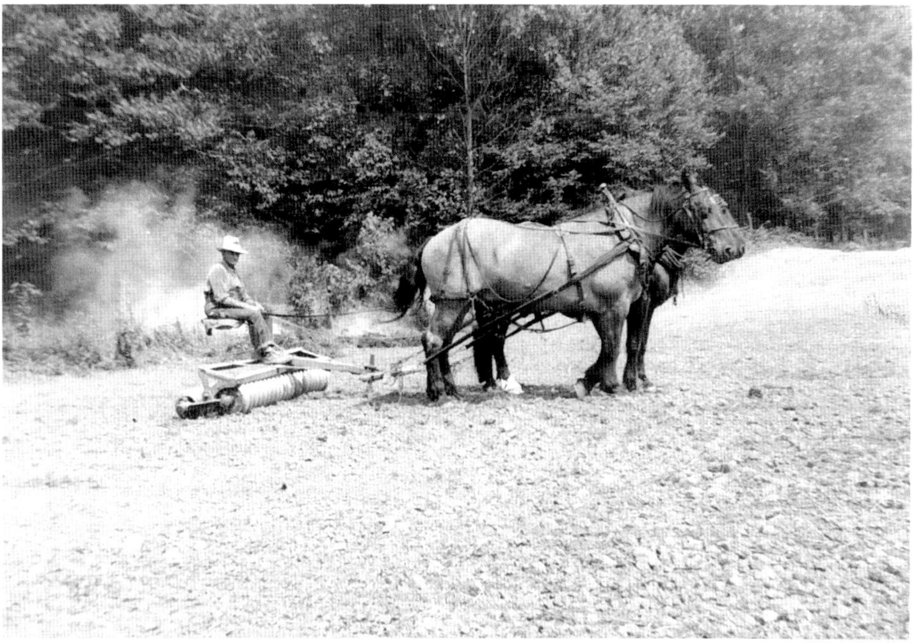

and cream into the cooler and run cold water through the separator to rinse it out. One of the trusted inmates will thoroughly wash the separator—Ray says that's one chore we don't have to do. It is one advantage of working at a place like this. Another inmate will churn the cream to make butter—we don't have to do that either. Still another man will fetch the skim milk and take it to feed to the pigs. Ray says, "It's the law—all of 'ems livin' here on the county 'at can work at all hasta work at somethin'." He says it might be milking, shelling corn, gathering eggs, feeding the ducks or chickens, fattening up some steers. And able-bodied men do field work as needed.

"It's good fer 'em." Ray says. "Elsewise they'd eat as much as if they was working and then jest set around and get constipated."

In the house the women peel potatoes, cook, bake, wash up the dishes; wash, iron, and mend clothes; help Cora with the cleaning. Women or men work in the gardens and orchard.

The home has two teams of work horses; two of the men take care of the teams and drive them on any job they're needed for. But inmates don't drive the tractors; that work is just for the hired hands.

The home has two tractors—a big, metal-lug-wheeled International Harvester tractor—Ray drives that one—and a smaller, rubber-tired Farmall.

That's the one I'm to drive.

Ray gets me started. After gassing up the Farmall at a little white building across Infirmary Road, Ray shows me how easy it is to start the tractor. You just turn an ignition key, for this tractor has a self-starter just as an automobile has. There's no need to turn a crank or spin a flywheel. Ray lets me drive the Farmall up and down the road, stopping, starting, turning, until I get the feel of it. It's a little different from driving a car, but not too different.

Then he starts the big tractor and gets up on it. He motions me to follow him on the Farmall. He drives slowly along the road, turns right across a small bridge over the county drainage ditch, and enters a field. The field has been plowed, and more than half of it has been smoothed and pulverized somewhat with a disk harrow; that harrow sits where the disked part ends. On a small part of the disked land the remaining clods have been broken up and the soil further smoothed, in final preparation for planting, with a spring-toothed harrow. That harrow sits where that "fitting" job has been left off. Fitting the soil, making it ready for planting—that's what Ray and I will be doing today.

Ray drives the big tractor up beside the spring tooth and says, "Boy, stop there. Let me up on the Farmall."

I get off it, and Ray maneuvers the little tractor in front of the harrow, gets off, hitches the tractor to the spring tooth, and remounts the Farmall. "Now, Boy, watch how this works." Off Ray goes, dragging the harrow. I watch as the harrow smooths a swath of the lumpy earth. Ray drives to the other end of the field, turns and comes back toward me, smoothing another part. He lets me try, but he walks alongside "just in case." The driving feels different with a load attached. But oh! It does feel good—I am finally working the soil, working the land!

When Ray is satisfied that I'm doing all right, he mounts the International and drives off across the field toward the disk harrow. Somehow he manages to roll a cigarette as he drives—that's a neat trick! He hitches the International to the disk harrow and resumes disking where he'd left off a couple of days before.

The early morning drizzle has stopped; the soil, though still damp on top, is dry enough to work. Ray and I keep working steadily most of the forenoon. Then I come to a low place in the field that is considerably wetter than the rest. My tractor's tires get over most of it without slipping, but the teeth of the harrow catch in the mud. Feeling the drag, I give the tractor more gas, but it's no use. It stalls out. I start it up and try again. No success. I stand up and wave both arms at Ray. He sees me and walks over to rescue me.

"Yuh gotta go out on a chain, Boy, t' yank that harrow outta there. That's why we keep this chain under the seat."

After unhitching the Farmall, Ray hooks the chain from it to the harrow, leaving loops of chain on the ground. Then, as he drives ahead, the chain straightens out to its full length. The tractor strains at the tug of the mired harrow, but Ray gives just enough more gas at the right moment to drag the spring tooth out of the low spot. Ray stops, backs her up, jumps down, unhooks the chain and hitches the tractor directly back to the harrow as before, ready for me to continue.

"Yul probably need to do that ever time yuh cross that mucky draw."

I nod.

Ray squats down on his haunches in the low spot, sticks his hand in the mud and pulls up a piece of red tile. "I suspected this—a broke drain tile. That's why it stays so wet here. We'll hafta replace it when we get time."

Ray pulls out his pocket watch. "Nearly noon. Guess we better haul our asses up t' dinner."

***

Dinner is great—country-fried steak, boiled potatoes, home-baked bread with fresh-churned butter, and blackberry pie. At each place is a small dish of lima beans swimming in milk and butter. I never had seen lima beans fixed that way—at home we just ate them plain or with just a little butter. I notice Ray make a funny face at them, but he eats them anyway.

After dinner, as we're heading back out to the field, he complains, "They always fix the vegetable in milk around here—what kinda way is that t' fix butter beans? They oughta fix 'em with some meat—streak-a-lean or fat-back."

I'd never heard of Ray's way of fixing them either, and I'd never heard lima beans called butter beans. But I don't say anything to all that.

I change the subject. "Ray, who drove the little tractor before I came here?"

"Since we lost our other hand to the army, sometimes Boss comes out to drive the small one. He's the one did that bit of fitting with the spring tooth in the field we're working on now. He really likes to keep his hand in, but usually he can't be spared from his other work. He's got a lotta book work to do, and he likes t' be around the house when we're out in the field in case some ruckus breaks out that Missus can't handle by herself. Usually she can—she uses her smarts real well and talks folks down when they get riled up, so she don't need so much muscle. Boss the same way. He don't lay a hand on any of them old folks lessen he absolutely hasta. But most of the time things are peaceable up t' the house. Jest once't in a while one of 'em's mind goes outta gear and makes 'em do crazy things that could hurt somebody. Then one of us hasta step in and stop it."

We continue our field work. Ray is right—I do have to go out on a chain a few times. I do it all right once and feel pretty smart. But the next time I hurry too much and don't get the chain hooked securely to the harrow. Off I drive, dragging the chain but leaving the spring tooth still stuck in the mud. Ray happens to see me and he yells over to me, "Don't waste time! Get it right the first time, Boy!" He almost sneers that word, Boy, and I feel the sting. I wish he would call me Will.

By chore time Ray has finished disking the field and I've gotten most all of it harrowed with the spring tooth. I would have finished the fitting but for getting hung up in the muddy draw part and having to go out on a chain so many times. Anyway, next time I'll knock off the rest of it fast, now that I know what I'm doing, and Ray says we can get our oats planted there soon, weather permitting.

***

At evening chores, I'm just finishing milking my second cow when I hear Ray cussing out one of the old men.

"Damn it t' Hell, Farley, yer just fooling around with that cow! That's not milking. That's just stripping without milking. You ain't got but two or three cups of milk in that pail, when you oughta have at least three quarts. Whatsa matter? You afraid to pull hard on those teats?"

Farley backs away from Ray's wrath, looking fearful and muttering under his breath.

Ray yells on, “Boy, yuh finished there? Get over here. See if you can get some more outta this one!”

“I’ll try,” I say as I pick up my stool and go to take the bucket from Farley.

Farley mutters slowly to me, “Watch out...she kicks.... She’s...a mean... son-of-a-bitch.”

I mouth thanks to him for the warning, while wondering to myself how a milk cow can be a son of anything. This cow is small and dark reddish in color almost all over, with only a couple of small white patches. I have no idea what breed or mixture she is, but she’s unique in our herd and I know I’ll have no trouble recognizing her. I sit down and feel her udder. It feels swollen with milk (as well as this greenhorn can tell). I start pulling on her front teats, just like I do with my other two cows. At the first pull, she kicks my leg and the bucket! Most of the milk Farley had gotten out of her spills onto the floor.

I stand up, pulling my stool out. I grab the bucket, right it, and put it back out of the way. I haul off and kick that red cow in the flank, as hard as I can!

She jumps, turns her head toward me, and gives me a startled look, or what I take to be a startled look. I keep staring her right in the eye as I reposition the stool, the bucket, and myself. I grab those two front teats and squeeze, squeeze, squeeze. The milk comes, the cow stands quietly, and I continue with no more trouble from her. I believe we have come to an understanding—she’ll stand still and I’ll milk her out completely. And I do.

I get a third of a pail of milk, and when I feel her bag again, it’s no longer tense and full. Ray comes over to see what I have in the pail.

“That’s more like it. Farley, ain’t yuh ashamed of yerself? Look what this new boy got outta her! Yer off the milking crew, starting right now.”

As Farley leaves the barn, he doesn’t really look to be ashamed, and I wonder if he had planned his escape from milking chores and is secretly gloating.

But Farley was right about that cow’s kicking. Maybe he just didn’t know that one good kick back would fix her meanness. I didn’t know it myself; it was just an angry reaction on my part, not a reasoned action.

Ray says, “From now on, Boy, yul milk this one too.” He feels her udder. “Yul probably get even more milk after she’s been milked out completely like this a few times.”

***

Supper tonight is much like dinner—a meat (ham this time), fried potatoes fixed from the boiled ones left over from dinner, carrots swimming in milk and butter. But instead of pie, the dessert is what they call "sauce". Tonight it's canned peaches, but it could have been plums, berries, rhubarb sauce, applesauce, or some other fruit or compote. There's cream to pour onto the fruit or into coffee. I don't drink coffee, so I ask if I might have milk instead. Cook says of course and right away fetches a pitcher of it from the kitchen. This is the first fresh unpasteurized milk I've ever drunk. It tastes good, not too different, except that it's whole milk and I'm used to partly skimmed. But I don't say anything, as I think Cook would have to go all the way down to the basement cooler to get any skim milk. That's if there's any of it left from our morning separating that's not already been sent for hog swill.

***

Now it's after supper, and it's still quite light because of the wartime daylight saving decree. I decide to explore a little before sitting down to note my first day's experiences for the senior thesis I have to write.

I cross the road and walk down to the field we fitted today, just to get some extra satisfaction from what I'd accomplished. I walk back along the road on the field side of the county drainage ditch. I pass a small plot which is overgrown with last year's tall dead weeds and which shows new green growth coming along amid them; I wonder what that plot is for. I go on to a graveled lot in front of the toolshed. That shed, open on one side, is where we park the tractors at night. It also serves as the garage for the truck and car. Various pieces of farm machinery that are not in use just now are parked there also, but I don't know what each is for. A few of the machines have long tongues so those must be for use with the teams of horses. Many have short tongues for use with tractors.

I go over to look inside a second big barn. It is generally like the dairy barn outside, but on the inside the main floor is mostly just a big open area. It lacks the stanchions and gutters of the dairy barn, and instead of ordinary horse stalls there are several box stalls along one wall. Three Hereford steers are in the open area for fattening. Ray had told me earlier that most of the beef herd is already out on pasture. That had surprised me, because I'm used to spring coming late in Cleveland. But down here, away from cold Lake Erie, spring is further advanced and there is already some grass for the cattle.

I climb up a ladder to the hay mow. There is no hay in it. Instead, the mow holds a bobsled, two cutters, a carriage, several buggies, and various household items—furniture, old butter churns, kerosene lanterns. Those sorts of things. It takes me a minute of wondering till I figure out that all of these things, once useful, must have been left over from "the old days" at the home, or perhaps were brought with people to the home and, too good to throw away, were kept here, gathering dust.

I could spend hours here looking at these old things, but it is beginning to get dark outside and it certainly is dark now in the closed-up mow. I go back outside and continue my stroll past the little locked shed where we gassed the tractor this morning and along the fence of the near pasture.

I peer at the dairy cows, trying to pick out the two Holsteins I milked today. I'm not sure which ones they are. But the red cow that kicked me—I'd know her anywhere. I wonder if she recognizes me as the guy who kicked her back! I hope so, as I don't want any trouble with her, ever again.

As I stroll farther along between the pasture fence and the drainage ditch, out of the corner of my eye I catch a glimpse of a muskrat down in a muddy, weedy part of the ditch, just above the water line. I think it has spied me too, for it slips into the water with a very soft *blip-ip* and swims away. A nice end to my first full day here. I turn back to where I can cross the ditch and Infirmary Road to go back to the big house.

Dad was right in a way—I'm too tired to write a word about my day, but I find that I'm too wound up not to write. And so I do write.

THE BATTLE OF THE BUGS

Boss and Missus were on a rampage yesterday. Especially Missus.

It's those bedbugs. You know how they are. No sight of them all day, but when the lights are turned off at night, they squeeze their thin bodies through the slimmest of cracks in the old wood floors and chairs, slip out of the hollow legs of the iron bed frames. Then they climb up the outside of the frames and into the bedclothes. There they bite, bite, bite the poor old folks who are trying to sleep.

When the sleepers stir a bit, and well before dawn, it's back into hiding for the bugs—back to the cracks, the hollow bedframes, the insides of mattresses and pillows. The bugs leave a souvenir of their visit—a row of bloody little bite holes in each victim's skin.

Here at the County Home—the poor farm—the bugs hadn't gotten into the staff quarters yet, but they were everywhere in the wards...and Boss and Missus wanted the biting of their people stopped.

There was no work in the fields yesterday for Ray and me or for the old men who work with us. We were needed at the Home's main building for a more important job. We'd been recruited for the all-out assault on the bedbugs.

Missus had the battle all planned out and put her plan into action. While we hired hands were finishing the morning milking, eating our breakfast, and separating the cream, Missus had some of the inmates start up the extra boiler in the basement. That boiler is pressed into service when we butcher a hog and for the big laundry on Mondays. But this was Wednesday, and Missus had planned a new use for the boiler's steam. One man filled the boiler with water while others carried in wood and started the fire. The men filled the hog-scalding trough outside the basement window with cold water. Then they rigged a long extension pipe from the boiler through the window and ran the pipe end into the trough, just the way they would do for scalding a hog.

Meanwhile, other able-bodied inmates, men and women, were hard at work in the sleeping wards. From every bed the women stripped the bedclothes and carried them outside to the yard. Next they carried every mattress and pillow out to a plowed but not yet planted garden plot. There they emptied all the corn shucks into a big pile and then brought the empty mattress and

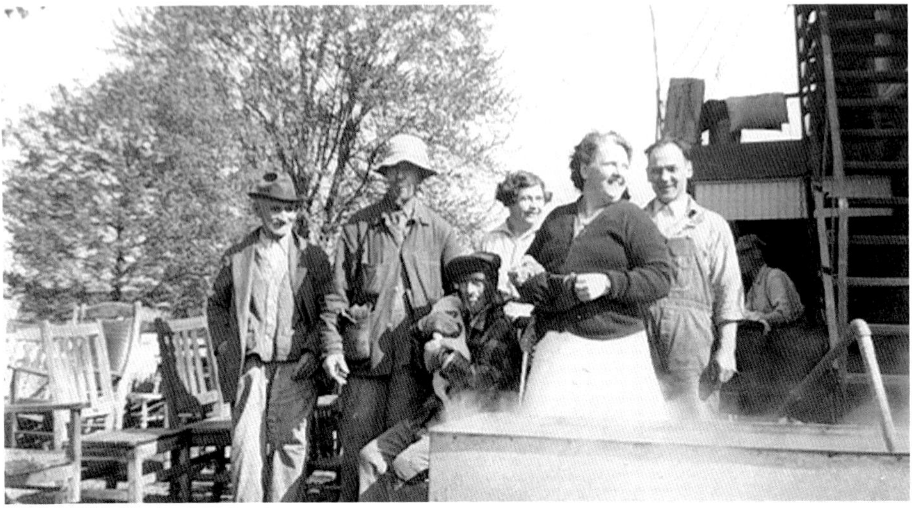

pillow ticks back to the bedclothes pile in the yard for later laundering. The old men took the metal beds apart. They picked up every piece of every bed, and every last old wooden bench, straight chair, and rocking chair, and carried them outside to the vicinity of the hog-scalding trough, lining them up in ranks like soldiers.

Everything was ready. As soon as the old folks had eaten their breakfast, the battle began. Boss reached through the window and turned the valve on the boiler so that the steam could run through the pipe into the hog trough. Soon the water was very hot. The folks carried buckets of it to the wards and poured the steaming water on the old wood floors. Any bedbugs hiding in floor cracks were cooked on contact. I could hear Missus yelling orders to Cora, "Make sure they hit all the cracks. Wipe out every last bug!"

Out at the trough, Ray and I got to work.

"How're we gonna do this, Ray?"

Ray picked up the first straight chair in line by its back, pointing the seat down, and held out the legs toward me. "Grab a-holt them top two legs. Now push the chair partway down in the water. Hold it there. And see yuh don't get yer hands in and scald 'em!"

"O. K., done. Now what?"

"Jest. . . ho-o-old it a minute. Then let go when I tell yuh."

Ray grabbed a hay fork and pushed down a bit on the back of the chair. "Now let go."

I let go, and Ray pushed the chair all the way down in under the boiling water and held it down with the hay fork. We watched as the bugs exited the chair's cracks, were cooked, and floated to the surface. As Ray then let up his pressure on the fork, the wooden chair floated up.

"Now, how're we gonna get that thing outa there without burning our hands, Ray?"

Ray answered by turning the fork over and catching underneath the chair back by the fork's tines. Then he said, "Take that baling hook and catch it a-holt that stretcher."

I didn't want to act too dumb in front of Ray, so I had to guess what a stretcher was. I guessed right—it was the rod connecting the chair legs—and I hooked over it.

"Not that way, Boy," Ray gruffed. "Turn the hook over and catch it up under the stretcher, so's we can haul up the chair without chancin' havin' the hook slip off!"

"Okay, I get it." I tried to act nonchalant as I obeyed him, but I felt bad, showing myself stupid before Ray after all. I bet he never before dipped chairs to debug them, so how did he know so well how to do it, when I hadn't a clue? It's no wonder he called me "Boy" that sneering way. He made me feel about as small as a bedbug! Then I thought (I don't know why) of my cousin Daniel in the Battle of the Bulge, with all that big stuff bursting all around him and over him. Daniel must've felt as small as a bug, but terrified too, for he knew he'd likely die, just before he got his. Not like these stupid bugs before they got theirs.

After Ray and I had fished the chair out of the steaming bug soup, Boss sent it to dry on the lawn in the sunshine. We went on dipping the other chairs and the benches. The rocking chairs had to be double-dipped, once with the seat pointed down and then with the seat pointed up, since the long rockers stuck clear up out of the water on the first dipping.

Next came the iron bed pieces. The hollow, U-shaped sections forming the legs at the head and foot were filled with bedbugs. We had to be careful not to splash the steaming water on us as we lowered the heavy iron pieces into the vat. Then, as we hooked and lifted the pieces out, we had to take special care not to be burned by the scalding, bug-laced water running back out of the hollow legs. It was dangerous work, but satisfying as well, our doing in those biting bugs that way. It was hard work too, so Boss from time to time spelled Ray at the trough, and then me.

Missus, in her old gray wool work sweater, was in her element. She was smiling, even laughing as she bustled about from the wards to the vat to the lawn, making sure that no piece of ward furniture escaped the steam bath. Boss teased her, "I never heard tell of a general laughing the troops into battle!"

Soon all of us were laughing—laughing so much that we got too weak to hoist the bed frames out of the trough and had to lean against the wall to keep from falling down, but we recovered and continued our work.

Finally, we finished! The water's surface was a solid sheet of boiled bug bodies. Boss reached for the valve to turn off steam to the trough.

Just as he did, Rebecky came racing up, wringing her hands sore and red, the way she always does when folks misbehave and she has to tell on them. "Marty snuck his chair away. He's settin' under the front porch, hidin' it. It never got dipped, not at all!"

"Poor Marty," Missus said. "He thinks we mean to harm it. Thank you, Rebecky. I'll go try talking him out of there first. If that don't work, I may need some strong-arm help to get that big lug to turn his rocker loose."

In two minutes, Missus, diplomat as well as general, returned in triumph, carrying the chair herself, followed at three paces back by a worried-looking Marty. "I told him I'd take good care of it myself," she whispered to Boss. "I think he trusts me, a little bit at least."

Boss and I dipped the chair, but Missus kept one hand close to it all the time, hoping Marty wouldn't get too upset. She also kept one eye on Marty, in case he would try to grab his chair out of the boiling water. Ray, the strongest of us all, stood close by and kept both of his eyes on the anxious, wild-eyed giant. But the dipping went all right, with no interference from Marty. Missus said, "Now you can have your chair back. Take it out to the lawn. Put it in the sun to dry out." Marty did, but right away he sat down on the still damp rush seat to rock back and forth, back and forth, the wildness draining from his eyes as the water drained from the chair.

Then Boss did turn the boiler valve, keeping the steam in the basement for laundering the bug-infested bedclothes and ticking. Boss and Ray and I, bone-weary, sat for a while on the benches behind the house. We rubbed our aching arms while we watched a huge bonfire rise from the garden plot—they were burning the corn shucks they'd emptied from the mattresses and pillows. I could picture the incineration of the bugs that had hid out in the shucks—could see in my mind's eye the blood-swollen bug bodies popping and curling, the blood turning black—though I was much too tired to walk down to see the burning at close hand. But not Missus—she skipped off gleefully to supervise the annihilation by fire of the last of the enemy. At least, she thought it was the last.

But unbeknownst to Missus, or to any of us that day of the battle, there was a fifth column inside the second-floor women's ward. Well, not exactly a fifth column; actually, it was just one little woman. As they say, never underestimate the power of one person, even if she stands only four feet tall and lives in a world of her own construction, even if some people call her Crazy Fanny or Funny Fanny or any number of other demeaning names.

I had gotten some of Fanny's history from long-time staff members who had been here at the Home when Fanny first arrived. It seems that Fanny's parents for many years had kept their mentally ill daughter naked and half-starved in their cellar. I imagine that, during that time, Fanny had made herself a promise—had vowed never to go hungry again. She had learned to push up the heavy outside cellar door when all were asleep in the house, slip outside, and then crawl through a window into the kitchen. There she would help herself to bread before sneaking back to the cellar, like a bedbug crawling back to its crack after taking its blood meal.

Eventually, a neighbor, passing the farmhouse late at night, witnessed the naked ghostwoman's activities and reported them to the authorities. The sheriff came with a court order and took Fanny away to the County Home to live decently at last. There, clothed and among friends, she had ample meals, including all of the home-baked bread she could eat.

Still, the memory of her long deprivation must have stayed with her, for at every meal of every day Fanny slipped two pieces of bread into her apron pocket, taking them to the ward to eat between meals or to keep hidden away, "just in case." By now, we thought we knew all of her hiding places, as there is not much privacy in a ward of twenty-five women. The ward cleaners often had found and removed pieces of bread from chinks and crannies, from under her mattress, from inside her pillow case. But Fanny's craftiness had been honed to a sharp edge in twenty years of cold, darkness, and isolation in her parents' cellar: now she had found a new hiding place for bread—in the toes of her cotton stockings, the red-and-white-striped stockings she is so proud of and which she wears day and night for the whole week between Saturday baths. Some bedbugs had found a convenient hole in each stocking, crawled in, bit Fanny for their blood meal, and holed up in the bread. So the Wednesday of our all-out battle against bugs, these bugs were not discovered. From this small squad, the enemy had begun to breed a new army into existence!

No one knew of the bugs in the stockings and wouldn't have learned of them except that today, Thursday, Rebecky happened to see something. She saw Fanny pull off one of her stockings and from the toe retrieve a piece of bread and gobble it up. Well! Although Rebecky may not have known about the bugs in the bread, or that Fanny maybe ate a few bugs when she finished the bread off, Rebecky does know misbehavior when she sees it. Rebecky's hands started their wringing and she ran right off to tell Missus.

You know by now that Missus is a crackerjack thinker when it comes to solving problems. As soon as she found the remaining buggy bread in Fanny's stockings, she got right to work on the problem of wiping out for good the enemy's last stronghold. First she said, "Fanny, you never have to be hungry here. From now on, anytime you feel the least bit hungry or anxious, you go right to the upstairs kitchen door where Cook will give you bread. You eat it right then and there. Do you understand?" Fanny looked puzzled, so Missus said, "Come, I'll show you," and she led Fanny to the kitchen door and had Cook give her some bread.

"Anytime, Fanny, anytime," Cook said, echoing Missus. Fanny wolfed the bread; she seemed to understand.

Next, just in case Fanny didn't understand after all, Missus cut the toes right off the red-and-white-striped stockings. Fanny wears those stockings proudly even with the toes cut off, though they're not quite comfortable for her, but think of all those old folks sleeping through the nights to come, with nary another bite to disturb them, in those last comforting sleeps toward the final one.

DIGGING A GRAVE IN THE POTTER'S FIELD IN THE RAIN
SPRING, 1945

It's nearing planting time, but it's raining today for the third day in a row, the soil is soaked, and we can't go into the fields to plow or fit them. Anyway, an old man died in his bed last night. No one knew it till the five o'clock bell rang this morning. That's when the other old men in the second floor men's ward noticed he didn't get up, and when they took hold of him to shake him awake they found he was cold and stiff and dead.

(While half a world away,
legions of men are dying of
typhus, starvation,
cyanide gas, and hate.)

Adam and Don came to the upstairs kitchen door, where they asked Cook to fetch the superintendent right away. When Boss came out, still buttoning his shirt, they told him. Boss's face went into its worried, thinking look for just a minute. He looked out at the rain. Then he decided and his face relaxed. With all this rain, the hired hands and the able-bodied old men could dig the grave today. That would give them something to do rather than fixing fence again, and the dead man could be buried today before he began to stink.

Boss says, "If you fellas will just go back and pull old Ned's sheet and white coverlet up over his face fer now, then after chores and breakfast we'll bring up one of the boxes from the basement supply room and put him in it till the diggin' is done."

Don and Adam leave to do as they were asked.

Ray and I are passing through the kitchen on our way out to the barn and we hear it all. Boss tells us which men we should take for helping with the digging.

The dead man had no family and, although he had been at the County Home for some twenty years, he had no really good friends among the other old men, so there was no one to mourn him much. Still, some of the really old men are bound to be upset, Ned's death reminding them that they themselves haven't much time left. So the boss, a friendly and caring man, ties his shoe laces quickly and follows the two messengers up to the ward. Ray and I follow along too. Boss checks to be sure Ned really is dead and then he tries to soothe

the other old men's anxieties as best he can.

Because of the rain, the men who are too feeble to help with the milking or feeding have to stay inside to wait for the breakfast bell, so Boss suggests, "Why don't all you fellas just go set in the first floor men's ward, so you won't have to stay in the room with Ned's body?"

Most of the men do go on downstairs, but two of them say they'll sit with the dead man, as it's proper someone should and they don't much mind doing it. Ray and I head for the barn and Boss turns back toward his office in the staff quarters, saying, "I need to phone Doctor Crisp to come by and sign the papers so you can get on with the burying."

***

After morning chores and breakfast, we get our shovels and cross Infirmary Road to the county potter's field, a tiny, weedy piece of land lying alongside a tilled field. I didn't know until now what use this piece of land serves, as it has no gravestones or markers of any kind. Ray has been working and digging graves at the County Home for quite a few years; he picks a spot for digging where they haven't put anyone recently. Still, I'm wondering how many bodies have been put into that patch of earth during the hundred or so years of the Home's existence. I half expect our shovels to strike a rotting casket or even human bones.

There are the two of us hands and four of the inmates to do the digging. We take turns with the four shovels we have, while the cold northern spring rain comes down steadily. The rain soaks down into our cotton work caps and jumper jackets and merges with our sweat that is wicking up through the cotton fabric.

The wet clay down in the hole and piling up around the hole is sticky and slippery at the same time. It sticks to our trench shovels and has to be scraped off with the wide end of a mattock. It encases our shoes and the lower legs of our jeans. It gets onto our hands, the handles of the shovels, and onto the backsides of our jeans when we slide down into the deepening grave to take a turn with a shovel. The clay is heavy to lift; our backs and shoulders and forearms, though well-conditioned to usual farm work, begin to ache. We are cold, wet, muddy, miserable—all to bury a friendless old pauper we scarcely knew.

(While half a world away,
in the cold, wet, northern European spring,
other men are digging
the last mass graves of the war.)

By eleven o'clock we are down only four feet. I scan Ray's face, looking for agreement to stop there instead of going for the usual six-foot depth.

Ray explodes, "A fella hires on to do farm work and what kinda job they give him? Diggin' a damn grave in the rain!"

That decides it: we've dug far enough. We jam our shovels into the clay piled beside the grave and head for the house to get old Ned. Boss sees us coming and, after surveying our thorough muddiness, decides that he himself will take some dry old men to fetch the coffin, with Ned in it, down to us. So we hitch the stoneboat to the Farmall and pull it up behind the back steps of the men's ward. Then we wait under the eaves out of the rain, while Boss and the dry old men maneuver the coffin down the narrow stairs and onto the stoneboat.

Once we have hauled the box over to the grave site, we lower it down with ropes, unceremoniously, the ropes slipping in our muddy hands and our feet slipping in the mud. We shovel the clay into the hole and mound it up over the grave. No words at all are said aloud over old Ned, to mark his passing.

(While half a day's drive away,
in a rented hotel room in the city,
words are *said by an Army chaplain,*
and the Army, in dismal ceremoniousness,
presents a medal and an American flag,
in lieu of mortal remains,
to the mother of that young soldier,
my cousin Daniel, who'd been
blown apart in the Battle of the Bulge.)

The rain finally stops. Boss's young daughter, carrying a bunch of weed wildflowers, pushes through the tall, wet weeds. She tramps through the mud and puts the weed flowers on the mound.

(While half a world away,
in this spring of liberation,

weeds grow over the earlier mass graves
and, on the now quiet battlefield,
weeds take root in the far-flung, mouldering
bits of the young soldier's flesh, and grow, and
burst into bloom.)

MORPHINE

I'm a heavy sleeper. I didn't even hear the shot in the night.

One shot—that's all it took—and George Carson was dead. Dead on the hallway floor, in front of the gun cabinet. How he had managed to do it, weak as he was from the cancer that had spread throughout his body, was a mystery. How had he gotten through the heavy locked door between the first floor men's ward and the staff quarters? How had he opened the locked gun cabinet? How had he known where Boss hid the bullets and how had he loaded the pistol, all before he pointed the barrel to his temple and squeezed the trigger?

The first I knew of it was when the morning bell rang and I got up, pulled on my jeans, and was heading toward the bathroom.

I heard hushed male voices rising from the floor below. I leaned over the stairwell railing to look and listen. Boss and Ray, along with the chairman of the Upshaw County commission and the sheriff, were standing around George's body. Old Dr. Crisp, the Home's attending physician, was kneeling beside George. The doctor stood up.

I heard him say to Boss, "He's dead, all right. There's nothing I can do for him. I hate to lose a patient this way, to suicide. Okay if I use your office phone to call the coroner? By law, George's body will have to be taken to the morgue. The sheriff, here, could take it, but I'd rather have the coroner himself come here to fetch it."

"Help yourself, Doc. You know where the office is. I've already phoned George's niece to let her know. She's on her way over here with that mortician husband of hers."

Doc said, "Just don't let them, or don't any of you, disturb the body or anything around it. The coroner will finish his exam and release the body to them soon enough."

Boss went on, "It's good that we won't have to put George in the potter's field here, that he has some kin left to see to his proper burial. Too bad about his son dying out there in the Pacific. In the natural order of things, you expect the sons to bury the fathers, but this war's turned things topsy-turvy. Why, just last month, sick and weak as he was, George had us take him to the church for his son's service and then out to God's acre so he could be the one to toss the first shovelful of earth on his boy. I had to hold him up and help him some, but he did it all right!"

Just then another man appeared below, a man I'd never seen before.

"How did you get here so fast?" Doc asked him. "I haven't even phoned you yet!"

"Oh, the mortician phoned me as soon as he got the word. He knows I would have to be brought in before he could take the body. Now everyone step back and let me get a good look here. Has anyone touched the body?"

Boss said, "I did. When I couldn't get any pulse, I phoned Doc Crisp here, and the sheriff and commissioner. We've never had a suicide here, leastwise not since I've been superintendent. I wasn't sure who to call."

Doc said, "I examined George enough to verify that he was dead. Other than that, nothing's been disturbed."

Boss stepped over to the men's ward door, the door that George had somehow gotten through. Boss said, "When I heard the shot and got down here pronto, this door was closed, but it wasn't locked the way it should have been." Boss opened the door, looked and felt along the door jamb and all along the door's top, edge, and bottom. "No sign of any jimmying, but I didn't really expect that, since I'd found the door unlocked. I guess George must have got hold of a key somehow."

"Any chance the door was left unlocked by mistake?" the sheriff asked.

"No, I checked it myself, like I always do, last thing before I went up to bed."

"Could anyone else have gone through after that—say, Missus or Cook, for a last check on a sick man in there?"

"Not likely. Nobody's that sick just now, except for George; anyway, there was nothing more could be done for him last night. We'd already given him his allowed nightly dose of morphine for his pain."

"Then, how about the gun cabinet door? Had it been jimmied?"

"No, I checked that before you got over here. And there's no sign of a key in the lock or on the floor."

The sheriff checked the doors for himself, and then asked, "Is the gun cabinet kept locked ordinarily?"

"Oh, yes, all of the time," Boss answered, "except when I open it to get Ray a shotgun and shells to take out to the pasture for shooting a beef in the head before butchering it."

"You mean you butcher right out there in the field?" the commission chairman asked.

"Oh, no!" Boss replied. "Ray and the men just roll the beef onto a stoneboat and drag it back to the barn to butcher it there."

"And Ray brings the shotgun back at the same time?"

"Yes, and it's locked back up in the cabinet at once."

"So, who locks it up—you or Ray?"

Boss replied, "I do usually. If I'm not available, Ray gives or sends the gun in to Missus and she locks it up while Ray gets on with the butchering."

The commissioner hesitated a minute; it seemed to me that his lawyer's brain was working overtime. (Was he wondering what liability the county might be incurring, or the commissioners themselves in their oversight of the home?) Then he said, "I know the shotgun wasn't involved in this suicide, but a pistol was, from the same gun cabinet. It's the locking of the cabinet that I'm concerned about, and that unlocked door to the men's ward. By the way, where do you keep bullets for that pistol?"

Boss lowered his voice even more, but I thought I heard him say, "In the same gun cabinet, but way up high inside on a little hidden shelf. I'm the only one who knows where they are, except for Missus and maybe Ray."

I glanced down at Ray, who had said nothing all this time; I saw his jaw tighten at the mention of his name.

The commission chairman shook his head, as if to clear it, I thought. Then he said slowly, "I'll have to go over all this with the sheriff and the coroner here, and with the other commissioners—see what all of them think. But I see no need to call a special commissioners' meeting. We'll discuss it at our regular monthly meeting out here next week."

The coroner had said nothing more, but as he examined the body and its surroundings and took his notes, he seemed also to be listening intently to the questions and answers of the others.

***

A few minutes later, as Ray and I headed out to the barn for morning chores, I myself was full of questions. To me, right then, the biggest mystery was not how George did it, but why he did it.

"Ray, do you think George just felt like he had nothing to live for after his son died in the war?"

"I dunno. Anyways, this place is jest one big waiting-room for death. Maybe George jest thought, why wait? Why wait around with all these other old farts—jest get it over with."

"But George wasn't an old fart. Boss said he was only middle-aged, that he just was thin and looked so old because of the cancer."

"So what? All the more reason to check out! Besides, Doc didn't give him enough morphine. George hurt all the time from the cancer. How much pain can a man take anyways?"

"But why didn't Doc give him enough? Doc's a kind man. He doesn't want his patients to suffer."

"I dunno. I'm an outdoor man—I don't go into the wards unless I really hafta. But once I hadta, and I heard George moanin' over and over, 'Give me morphine! More morphine!' Most pitiful thing I ever heard. Ordinarily I'm a hard man, but to hear George cryin' so, that got to my guts."

I was thinking George could have gotten addicted to morphine and that's why he was pleading for it so. So I asked, "Ray, do you think George had got the morphine habit? Maybe that's why he got so pitiful crying for more—that, rather than the cancer pain?"

"Boy, you ask too many questions. Let's jest get the milkin' done."

***

Well, we did get on with the milking and our other chores, but all the time I couldn't get questions out of my head. I pondered over and over why Doc didn't give George enough morphine to control his pain. George was going to die soon enough anyway, so why not make him comfortable and pain-free in his last days, even if George should become addicted to the drug? I don't know the answer, but I guess that Doc hadn't been able to get enough morphine; maybe a civilian shortage developed because so much was needed to treat wounded servicemen.

Well, I kept thinking about the whole thing a lot the rest of the day, and the next day, and the next after that. After a while my mind got off of why George did it and turned back to the sheriff's and commissioner's dilemma—how George did it, getting through the locked men's ward door and the locked gun cabinet door. Even if one of those doors had been left unlocked out of carelessness, it was not likely that both had been, on the same night. And how would George have known about the bullets' hiding place? Or had he seen that particular pistol in there some time before that night, and somehow had got a hold of some bullets for that kind of pistol somewhere else? I wondered if anyone had checked to see if any bullets were missing from the hiding place, but I didn't ask as it wasn't my business to play detective. I wondered if George might have had some lock-picking skills no one knew about. I even wondered if some person or persons unknown might have helped George out, by leaving doors unlocked on purpose, say. Or smuggling keys to him, or supplying him with bullets or telling him the bullets' hiding place.

***

When all of the county commissioners came out the next week for their monthly meeting, the long dining table had extra places set for them for dinner, the way it always was when they came, and Cook put on an extra nice feed, as she always did when they came. At dinner there was no talk of George Carson's suicide. That afternoon after dinner Ray and I went back out to work in the fields while the well-fed commissioners held their meeting inside, and we knew nothing of what they said.

The subject of how George had carried out his suicide was never brought up again, in my presence, anyway.

I've figured out a slew of ways it could have happened, but I guess I'll never know which it was, or if it was some way I haven't even thought of yet. Some things I'll never know, no matter how badly I want to know them. Sometimes a mystery just has to stay a mystery. It's not like it were fiction—a story you could put down and close the book on, feeling satisfied. This really happened, to real people, and I don't know how it happened and never will. But I'll never stop wondering about it.

THE END OF THE WAR IN EUROPE
TUESDAY, MAY 8, 1945

Somehow, in this cold, wet, late spring we got our oats planted and made some headway on plowing and fitting for corn. But it's raining again today, so again we can't get into the fields to work. Besides, Boss has decided to help the war effort by selling off some of the food produced on the County Farm, rather than keeping it all here to feed the staff and the hundred or so inmates. So he has us put the high slat sides on the truck and load up a veal calf, a steer, and two fat hogs. Ray and Don and I climb into the cab and Ray heads the truck up Infirmary Road toward the paved highway. We're bound for the stockyards in Cleveland.

Ray holds it down to 35, the wartime speed limit, saving wear and tear on the truck's tires. With tire rationing so strict now, who knows when the Home can get any more? We get to the yards a little after noon, unload our stock, and get paid on the spot. I'm surprised at how small and strangely quiet the Cleveland stockyards are. Only two other trucks are unloading; both have loads as small as ours.

We're finished with our business and outside the gates by one o'clock. We stop at a cheap cafe for sandwiches and pie. The pie is terrible factory-baked stuff.

"Tastes like it was made with that *hy*-drogenated fat 'stead of lard," Ray grumbles.

We'd had our mouths set for some decent grub.

We head back south to the Home. Once there, we park the truck down by the toolshed and walk up toward the house. Farley, the old man who can never decide if he's tired or lazy, flops down on his bottom on the grass and asks, "Well,...didja... hear...the bells...ringing...in... *Cleve*land?"

"No. Why? What d'ya mean?"

"Well,...the war's...over...in...Europe!....What... d'ya... think...a that?"

***

What do I think about that? I'm glad it's over in Europe, of course, but I think it might be all over before I can get in it. It's been tough going in

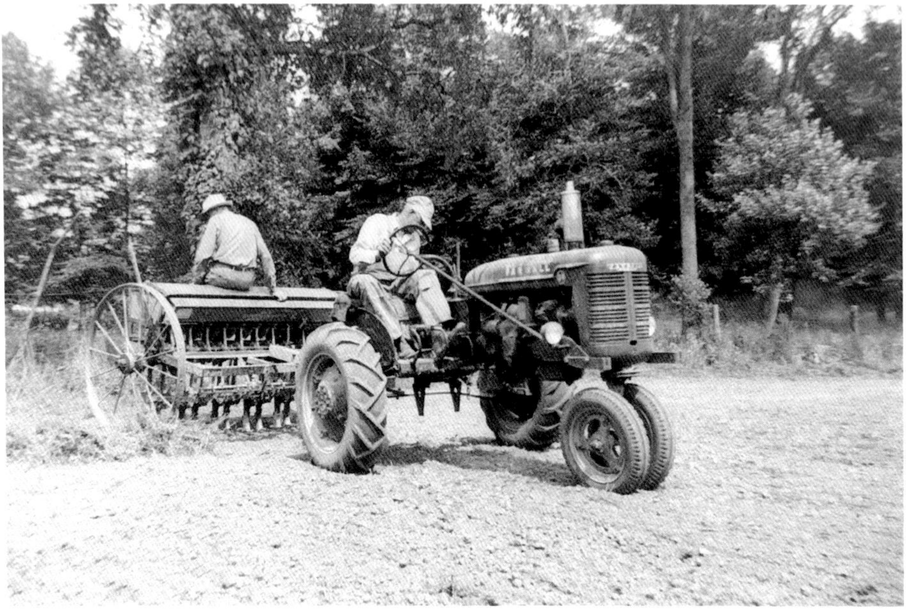

the Pacific, all right, but it is going, making progress, island by island. Still, everyone says in time we're going to have to invade Japan. That'll probably take a long time and a lot of men—so maybe I'll have a chance at it, a chance to fight for my country, fight like a man. Yeah, and a chance to get killed! Like George Carson's son.

I get to thinking, too, of Cousin Daniel. If they'd just finished it in Europe five months ago, he'd still be alive, but maybe not; suppose they'd shipped him over to the Pacific and he got killed by the Japs on some island there? He'd be just as dead.

Well, that's enough thinking—thinking about war and young men dying. It's chore time, a time for work, feeding the stock, squirting milk into pails, and in the big house, cooking meals, doing for the old folks. Now and then one of them dies here, but life mostly just goes on at this county home. For now, I'm part of this life. And for now, that has to be enough.

IMPORTANT HAPPENINGS

What a day this has been!

I got tickled at Ray this morning. We were out planting corn, and had stopped for a minute about eleven o'clock. We'd had just French toast for breakfast, and here it was still a whole hour till dinnertime, and both of us were already hungry. Then all of a sudden, out of the blue, Ray exploded.

"The eats a fella gets around here of a mornin' ain't worth a damn!" He crooked his little finger up in imitation of a lady putting on airs the way she might hold a teacup at a fancy party. "French toast! French toast! One little piece of fried bread—it's enough to choke up yer ass."

I had to stifle a laugh, as Ray was dead serious. I just nodded and said, "Yeah, I can feel my stomach rubbing up against my back bone." I'll never come close to Ray in the colorful comment department.

We finished our corn planting before dinner. The oats we'd planted earlier are up and growing well, and the hay and wheat are coming along fine. Looking out over the fields, I'd begun to feel like a farmer, though of course my part in all of this had been pretty small.

***

Cora was feeling poorly this morning and had to go and lie down awhile, so I was recruited to help serve the inmates' dinner. The rule is that staff waits table for the inmates' meals, so that all of the folks can sit down and eat together, without some having to wait on others.

In the basement there are two long dining rooms, one for men and one for women. Each room has two long tables. Meals are served family style, but someone is needed to pour coffee and bring in extra plates of bread during the meal. For this job I was assigned to the men's tables.

I was not quite happy with this indoor job. I thought it was not exactly men's work, but I pitched in without grumbling. Just before the bell was to ring for the meal, I was standing by with a big enameled pot of fresh, steaming coffee. Mrs. Clark said to go ahead and pour coffee into each cup and then go to the kitchen and refill my pot, to be ready for the next round of pouring. And I did.

As soon as the bell rang, two hordes of hungry folks came pouring down the two sets of six steps into the basement, men down one stairs, women down the other. Standing there with my refilled pot in hand, while the men seated themselves at the table I glanced over at the stairs the women had come down.

That's when I saw it, the sight of the last two old women slowly descending—the halt leading the blind! I blinked and looked again. It was true. A small, old, gimpy-legged woman held fast to the left railing with her left hand and tightly held the hand of the blind woman in her right. The halt stepped down one step with her left foot, then swung her stiff right leg around and down in an arc from her hip, almost kicking the blind in the process. The crippled woman positioned her right foot next to the left on the same step. Then she gave a slight tug to the blind woman's hand. The blind stepped down, very slowly and carefully, with one foot, then the other, feeling for the riser with the back of her heel and for the step with her slippered sole, before planting her weight on the foot. Thus they proceeded, step by careful step, until they reached the level floor, where the halt led the blind to her place and helped to seat her.

I turned back to my job, as the coffee disappeared fast from the men's cups and the men kept asking for more, please. The bread plates also needed refilling several times. When the men had finished their meat, potatoes, and vegetables, with coffee and bread, and had eaten their pie with more coffee, they continued to ask for more bread, which most of them dunked in their coffee, until they were satisfied at last. I was kept quite busy. And I always got a thank you, each time I refilled a cup. I'd like to see such politeness in the "outside" world.

***

After dinner we turned to the big garden. I had finished fitting it, and Boss had bought a slew of cabbage plants from a farmer down the road who had cold frames and who specialized in nursery stock. This afternoon we got the men to plant all those little cabbages. Ray said we grew so many so we'd have plenty for cole slaw and cooked cabbage and to make sauerkraut later on. I looked forward to seeing how they made and kept sauerkraut, as at home we just open a tin can of it already made; it had never occurred to me to ask Dad how to turn cabbage into sauerkraut. Dad had told me that Germans like to eat a lot of it, and that's why German soldiers in the Great War often were called "Krauts." I know we sometimes call the Nazis "Krauts" in this war too.

While we were standing around talking I told Ray I'd read in my high school biology book that sauerkraut is a good source of vitamin C. And that, back in the old sailing days, German sailors didn't get scurvy, the vitamin C deficiency disease, like the British sailors did, because the Germans always carried and ate sauerkraut on their voyages.

Ray just snorted, "Scurvy! Scurvy! That's just scurf. That's all it is!"

I didn't argue with him. When he held his own opinion so strongly—well, I knew it was no use to argue. Just the same, I knew I was right. Ray knew a lot from experience all right, and he could figure out a lot of things, but I'd begun to see he hadn't much use for book learning.

***

Now it's after supper. Boss has let me use his desk in the office this evening. I finished the pencil draft of my high school senior thesis yesterday, and tonight I'm writing out a fair copy in ink. I'll take it home Sunday on my day off, and my mother's promised to turn it in for me Monday, the due date, to the English teacher at school. The thesis is about my farm experience so far; it's for completing my graduation requirements. Dad thought I wouldn't get it written at all, but I did it. I'm proud of that. Proud that I had the will power to write something down every evening, no matter how tired I was at the end of the work day.

Boss comes into the office. "Just thought I'd drop in and see how you're comin' along with your copyin'."

"I'm almost done—just one page to go. Do you need your desk back now?"

"Oh, no. Carry on." Then he asks, "Bet you're glad to be gettin' that paper out of the way, so you won't have to be writin' every evening after this, eh?"

"Well, yes, I'm glad to have the thesis finished. But I'm going to keep on writing every evening this summer, on my own. That way, along with my thesis, I'll have a complete record of my whole spring and summer farm work. Besides, I've gotten to like putting things down on paper, seeing how well I can tell about things. Like today, Ray and I had some trouble with the planter. The outlet on one of the hoppers that hold fertilizer kept getting stopped up, so the fertilizer wouldn't feed down to the ground. I'll write how Ray tried to find the problem and fix it permanently there in the field, and when he couldn't, he just put me t' walk alongside and watch, and t' holler, "Stop!" every time the fertilizer stopped feeding down. Then Ray would work a wooden stick around in the fertilizer hopper to dislodge the clog. Then he'd go on as before, till it stopped feeding again. By that start-and-stop way of doing, we were able at least to finish the job—got the corn planted today. Later on when there's time to look at the problem more closely, I'll try to write down what had gone wrong and why, and how it could be fixed for good."

Boss smiles. "Sounds like a good idea. It'll be like you're writin' your own private 'Owner's Manual and Troubleshooting Guide' for each farm machine you learn to use.

"By the way, our next big job here will be the hayin'. The hayin' tools usually don't give us any big trouble—the mower knife blades have to be kept sharp, of course, and once in a while a knife section breaks and has to be replaced. If it comes to that, Ray can do that right here on the farm. He can show you how. The hayrake's never given us much trouble. The loader either. But hey! You don't even know what I'm talkin' about until you see all those tools on the job!"

Boss seems to be wound up, and he goes on, "Our next big job after the hayin' will be cuttin' and bindin' the oats and wheat. There, the binder's knotting problems could make a whole thesis all by themselves!"

"I'm looking forward to all of that, Boss. But right now, I've got to get this thesis copied and turned in!"

"O.K., I'll quit jawin' and leave you to your copyin'. Good night."

"Good night, Boss."

He leaves, and I copy off the last page. I've finished something. It's an ending.

When I go down the road to take the bus back home for my high school graduation in mid-June, and walk across that stage and they hand me my diploma, that will be another ending.

I'm beginning to see it clearly—life is a series of endings, up to the last one. But then, it's a series of recurrences and continuations, too, because, after graduation's over, I'll be getting on the bus again, to come back here. When I come walking up Infirmary Road toward the Home, Henry will spy me, as he always does when I come back after my Sunday off; he'll come running across the lawn toward me on his short legs with that humping gait of his, and he'll be smiling his big creased smile and yelling, "Boy heim! Boy home!" in that odd mixture of German and English he speaks. When I get back here, the haying will be continuing, and the war in the Pacific, most likely. The seasons will roll on and, as Boss said, we'll cut and bind the grain. Later on, the hired threshing crew will come in and thresh the oats and wheat, and all those seeds and plants we've put in the ground lately—in time they'll yield their bounty. We'll have beans, cabbage, tomatoes, and a whole lot more, all fresh from the garden, and the women will put up the excess in cans for winter. They'll put the root vegetables down in the root cellar, and they'll make sauerkraut, cucumber pickles, and chow-chow. The silo and corn crib will be filled.

The lives of the staff and inmates will go on, too. We all have our stories stored away in our minds, and we keep adding to them, a little bit each day, even when it seems like nothing important has happened. Maybe it's how you think about what's happened that makes it important or not. Like today: was the problem with the planter important? Was it important that I saw with my own eyes the halt leading the blind? Was one happening more important than the other? I don't know. I guess I'll have to think a good bit more about that.

When the folks here tell their own stories, they'll each have to decide what's important enough to tell. And what to leave out. But this I know: I want to hear those stories.

PART TWO

Their Own Stories

ADAM IN LOVE

I had wanted to learn to work horses, just to say I'd done it, not that I didn't see the great advantages of tractors. So one day when we weren't slated for field work Ray picked out about the simplest work for me to learn on—cultivating the big vegetable garden. He had Don show me how to put the harness on the gray horse and hook onto the one-horse cultivator. I ran it down between two rows of string beans, rooting out the weeds, the horse ahead doing the pulling and me walking behind, trying to manage the lines and at the same time holding to the two handles of the cultivator, trying to guide it. I must've looked pretty funny. I know I felt awkward, as well as afraid I'd lose control and root up some beans. That probably would've given the men a good laugh at the expense of the greenhorn, me. The gray knew what he was doing, and I caught on pretty fast, and so we worked on without any major disaster.

We finished the rows of beans and moved on to the other vegetables. Meanwhile, Ray put the old men to work pulling out the weeds by hand within the rows that the cultivator couldn't get to. As I came to the end of one row and stopped a bit to wipe the sweat off my face, old Adam called out to me, "Boy, look here. I show you dis."

"What, Adam? Oh, I see you're cutting a few good parts out of those old gunny sacks. What's that for?"

"You watch. See, I fold up piece, make square. Put four square in pile, make t'ick pad. I make two t'ick pad, one for each knee. Now watch some more. I take dis twine, tie 'cross pad, 'round behind leg 'bove knee. 'Round an' tie below knee too. Same other knee. So! All set weed on knees. Nice trick, eh?" Adam grinned.

"Know where I learn dat trick, Boy? I tell you. Fifty year on knees, weed onion in muck ground."

"Where's that, Adam—the muck ground, I mean?"

"Foxton. 'Over to Foxton,' dey say 'round here. Dey say just big swamp dere once, lo-ong time ago. No one want dat land. You own it, dey put tax on it way down for you. Den some smart guy say drain it—get rid of skeeters, get rid of fever. So dey do it. Turn into best damn land to grow onion, celery, all high-price crop. Den dey put tax way up on it! Hah-hah!"

"So that's where you worked, Adam, before you came here?"

Adam's eyes broke into a smile. "'Fore I retired to here," he corrected me. "Dey make me retire, say I'm too old for work. But only seventy den. Eighty now. An' you see me weed today. Best damn weeder of whole bunch here—fast, don't miss no weeds. You see old man weed like devil!"

He grinned a very wide grin. God!—his teeth—perfect! Adam is almost a giant. He still stands erect and proud at eighty. I could see he was just itching to get into the garden and show off to me how fast he could weed. He did just that. He weeded three rows to each one the next fastest man did, and weeded six rows while slow old Farley was finishing just one.

***

Now it's evening, after supper. The garden is clean of weeds, and some of the men are sitting around on benches on the lawn, smoking and relaxing. Adam, with his huge frame, takes up half a bench. I see that the other half of the bench is empty, which gives me a chance to join him for a spell. I want to learn more about his life. He still has an old-country way of speaking English, though he'd worked in the muck at Foxton for fifty years. I wonder why he came over here to the U.S., and why he stuck with that job for so long, when he seems so bright and gets along so well with everyone. With just a little prompting from me, Adam tells this story:

When I boy in old country, gypsy come to Papa's farm every spring. Same band gypsy every time. Camp on land down by river. I go every night long as dey dere—listen to violin play. I love dat moo-zick! Das when I first see her. I eighteen. She twelve, hair an' eye black like coal. Eye burn like coal too, right t'rough my heart. I want her. Want her for wife. I tell Papa, but he no like it. He say, "You no marry gypsy girl. You stay here on farm, work, find wife, settle down wit own people. Gypsy woman used to move on all-a time. She no be happy settle here. She only be happy wit her own people."

I don' tell Papa she only twelve. I can wait till she grow up, and Papa have time git used to idea an' mebbe change his mind.

Next spring gypsy come back. She t'irteen den. Still too young. Gypsy papa see me try talk to her. He pull her away. Set her brother to watch her.

Give me dirty look but don' say t'ing to me—'fraid I tell my papa kick dem off his land.

Next spring dey back again. She fourteen—girl become woman 'most. I tink old 'nough now. I so happy my heart swell.

Den I find she married already, to old gypsy man. She so young, why her papa marry her dat old man?

Gypsy violin sound so sad. I tink my heart break in two. I no can stay dere. I leave farm, leave old country. Come here. My cousin git me job in muck.

I like job. One day weed all day. One day tie up celery so center white. Dat kinda dumb job. No have to tink much 'bout work. So lotsa time tink of her—fifty year in muck, ten year here.

All-a time I hear moo-zick I tink of her. Radio play country song—I tink of her. Henry blow-draw-blow-draw on mout' organ—I tink of her. You play horn—I tink of her.

Sometime I tink of her—he still rise up, you know, Boy? Like young man! Like you, mebbe?

I no sad now. Healt'y old man, got clean bed here, good eats. An' plenty weed to pull! Hah-hah! But too many bosses, not enough paymasters! Hah-hah-hah!

I no complain. Had sixty year hear moo-zick an' tink of her.

Her. All-a time, Her.

HANNAH: IN HER OWN WORDS

I'll tell you this: I didn't come here peaceably. I fought them every step—that evil sheriff and his filthy deputy. And my own brother! He's the evil one got the court order. The nerve of him, coming along with them, trying to talk me into leaving my own home, and for what? The poor farm! How could he!

Why, we're quality folks. Not riffraff to end up on the poor farm. You see, my great-grandfathers, they came out to this county when it was new. Came all the way west from Connecticut and Massachusetts, across the mountains. They built this county. Cleared their land and planted it. Raised the best purebred horses, cattle, and sheep. Oh yes, they were thoroughgoing stockmen all right, their sons too, and fine, Christian gentlemen, all. In our family, we've had judges, preachers, headmasters, bankers. The movers and shakers of the county. My brother Bob's a druggist, has his own store. He's a deacon in the church, too, and *he* sent *me* to the poor farm. (Even a deacon can be evil, even your own brother.)

You see why I fought them, when they came to take me away. I was born in that house. Lived there all my forty years, there on the old homestead. You can't tell it now, but Great-grandfather Webster's original log house is hidden inside the walls. Under the wallpaper and lath and plaster inside, the clapboard siding outside. Of course, over the years there were three or four additions to the house, as the family grew. Four generations from Great-grandpa Webster to me. (Did I say we are kin to the great Daniel Webster?) My sisters and my brother grew up and moved away, but not me. I knew my duty. I took care of my parents till they passed to the arms of the Lord. Then I stayed on alone. I'd be there still, at home, if they had just let me alone. I liked living alone, with just my black cat.

But I wasn't lonely, oh no! You see, God spoke to me, all the time. He told me of all the evil in the world, how to recognize it. He once told me that my black cat was really the devil in disguise and that I had to strangle it and bury it under an apple tree. So of course I did—I had to obey God, and I couldn't have the devil living in my own home, could I? When my niece came to visit one afternoon, she missed the cat and asked after it. I told her what God said it really was and how I'd got rid of it. Do you know what that little pip-squeak niece of mine did? She went out and told everyone Aunt Hannah's gone religious batty!

Brother Bob came around to ask me was that true about the cat. "Of course," I said and I told him, "You get down on your knees and thank the Lord that devil cat's gone from this place!" He looked at me funny and left in a hurry. Then he came back with the sheriff.

So now you see how a person of quality like myself can end up living with the riffraff of the county at the County Home. County Home, that's what they call it now. Some home! Used to call it the County Infirmary. But we all know it's the poor farm. Brother Bob said not to fret, because he pays my way to live here, so I'm not really living on the county. Isn't that a laugh—paying to live on the poor farm? When I could live on my own place for nothing? Now that's batty. I'm not the crazy one.

Brother Bob said it's not good for me to live alone, that I need people around to talk with. Well! I don't talk to any of these people. Some of them are evil. Some are demented. Some are just stupid. So I talk with God, and with myself. That's the only way I can carry on a decent conversation around here.

Of course, I watch these people, watch for evil ways. I've got my eye on several of them, but especially on that Boy. That oh-so-innocent young face—it's a mask, you see. He's not fooling me. Or God. We know Boy is evil incarnate. There's that black wool sweater he wears on chilly mornings—that's a dead giveaway, you see. Black is the color of the devil. When the sun gets hot toward noon, Boy peels off that sweater, but that doesn't take away the evil, just divides it. Some of it stays in the boy, while some of it stays in the sweater. I wanted to wring Boy's neck, strangle him like I did the black cat. And I wanted to get my hands on that sweater!

***

Well, one day I saw Cora, the ward girl, come out of the house with that sweater. It was wringing wet; looked like she'd washed it out good. She pinned it on the line between the women's wing and the orchard.

I sidled up to her. "Good morning, Cora. How come you're putting out wash when it's not even wash day?"

Cora said, "Morning, Hannah. Oh, Boy was cleaning out some old milk cans with rust remover, and he got some of that strong muriatic acid on the sleeves of this sweater. Ate into the wool and made some holes. I had to wash it out right away with lye soap to stop the eating away."

"Oh." (I said that innocent-like to throw Cora off her guard.)

I waited till Cora went back inside. Then I snatched the sweater off the line. Carried it into the orchard. I had a short-handled trench shovel I kept hidden under the mulch around an apple tree, to use when I had to dig. I dug a hole there fast. Put that devil black sweater in the hole and covered it up with dirt, just as God told me to do.

I didn't think anyone had seen me digging and burying. But Rebecky had. She ran right to Missus and told her. They got Cora, and the three of them found my shovel under the mulch near the hole. Didn't they dig that sweater back up? Took it back in the house and washed it out again. Hung it back on the line. Flaunting the devil for all to see! Then they put Rebecky to watch me, that I didn't bury it again.

Imagine, they put that blabbermouth riffraff Rebecky to watch me! when I'd been watching her. She's another evil one, telling stories around.

***

What was I to do? My shovel had been taken away, and Rebecky was watching my every move. Then the voice of God spoke to me. God was everywhere, outside and inside my head, telling me what I had to do! God said, *Go to the garden alone. The tomato vines are evil, evil. Pull them up! Pull them up!*

With God urging me on, I pulled and pulled, faster and faster. Yanking up plants, throwing them up in the air, racing up and down the rows. Paying no heed to Rebecky. I was doing God's work, and I didn't care if she told.

Of course she did. First thing I knew, Ray was running after me, yelling, "Stop that, Hannah. Stop it now!"

But I didn't stop. I couldn't. God was saying, *Go on Hannah, pull, pull!* Who was I to listen to, that no-good hired hand Ray, or God Almighty? God, of course.

Next thing I knew, Ray had tackled me. Held me down on the ground. Boss and Missus came running up. Pulled my hands back of me and handcuffed them together. Rolled me up in a blanket. Tied the blanket tight with rope.

Oh, I fought them all right. I'm a strong woman, I am. But it was no use; they had me. A couple of old men brought a wheelbarrow down the garden path. Boss and Ray lifted me into it and trundled me away in it. I was all trussed up like a turkey readied for the oven. Me, a person of quality, doing God's work, and they treated me like that!

They didn't put me in the oven, of course. But they did lock me in a cell in the jail wing, and here I sit. I'd never seen a woman locked in here. These cells are supposed to be just for crazy old men who turn violent once in a while. Not for women of quality who obey all of God's commandments.

But I won't be kept in here long, thank God. I overheard Missus telling Boss, "We can't have Hannah in the women's wing anymore, and we can't keep a woman overnight in the jail wing with men. You've got to phone the sheriff right away."

That crazy old man in the next cell called out to me, "Hannah, they're fixin' to ship you off to the state asylum, sure enough."

But I know better. After all, the sheriff was called to bring me here. Now they're calling him to take me back home, back where I belong.

REBECKY'S STORY

Sure, I like to tell stories. But why would you want to hear the story of *my* life?

Well, O.K. Let's see. I was born, I guess. Then I growed up. And here I am.

That's about it.

What? Oh, my parents? Well, there was my daddy. Once he brought me a present. He had to go into Cleveland on business one day. He went on the electric interurban car. It don't run no more, now, you know, but then it did. He came back on the electric, too, all in the same day. It ran very fast, you know. Not like drivin' up there with horse and wagon. That could take all day.

Oh, the present! It was three monkeys. Not live ones, oh no! I mean three monkeys all made of cast iron, painted brown. They was sittin' together. One monkey had put his little hands over his eyes, so he couldn't see. Another one had his hands over his ears. And the third one had put his hands over his mouth. Them monkeys had names too. They was *See No Evil, Hear No Evil,* and *Speak No Evil.* Can you guess which name went with which monkey? I bet you can!

Daddy said he thought it was the perfect present for me; he always called me "Little Busybody." (That was his pet name for me, you know.) He said I was to take those monkey names to heart, and see no evil, hear no evil, and speak no evil, *ever.* So of course I obeyed Daddy.

To this day, I never do see no evil nor hear no evil. But sometimes I do see folks misbehavin'. I don't speak no evil of 'em, but I do report 'em so their misbehavior will be corrected right away. That's so's it won't have the chance of goin' on into evil.

Like once I saw Don kickin' up dust from his heels, high-tailin' it down Infirmary Road away from the Home. I ran to Missus right away and told her, "Don done gone down the road!"

Well! Missus told Boss, and Boss and Ray jumped in the car and took off after Don. But they didn't catch up to him. He must've jumped off the road into the neighbor's field and ducked between the corn rows. It was gettin' to dusk, and they couldn't spot him. Don made his getaway all right. He's the last person I would've thought would run away, much trusted and with a lot more common sense than most folks 'round here, but at least he didn't do no evil.

A week later Doc Crisp phoned Boss. Said Don had been workin' for him at his house over to Foxton, doin' yard and garden work and makin' repairs. Said Don was complainin' Doc was makin' him work too hard, and he wanted to come home. So Boss drove over there and fetched Don back.

'Nother time, when us women was doing some weedin' in the big garden, I spotted Marty way down at the far end. He wasn't supposed to be there. He was hidin' behind the raspberry bushes, and he popped his head up now-'n-again to leer at some woman and crook his forefinger at her, tryin' to get her to come down there to him. Now I know I don't have to explain to you what Marty had on his mind. Of course, I had to tell on him before his misbehavin' turned into evil doin's.

So Missus right away pulled all of us women weeders up to the near end of the garden and told us not to pay no heed to Marty. Then she ran over to where Ray and them was grindin' corn for feed, and she sent Ray down for Marty. Ray brought him up and around to the front porch of the men's wing and set him down in his rocker facin' the road, so's he couldn't see the women or try to lure them to him. Now you may be wonderin' how I know about this last part of Marty's story. Well, I couldn't just stay with the women in the garden, could I? I had to see how the story come out, so I snuck along after Ray and Marty just enough to see it, before Missus spied me and called me back.

What? You're askin' what *I* did in *my* life? Not what Don or Marty did in theirs? Well, I *thought* I just told you. I watched folks and listened to 'em, and I told on 'em when I had to! And I'm still doin' all that. It keeps me busy, 'cause there's so much misbehavin' goin' on.

I wouldn't have it any other way.

HENRY: THINGS I WAIT FOR

This is me, Henry. I'm a-gonna say a poem for you:

Hey! A-gonna thrwasha come!
Bay hoyee! Whi hoyee!
You wah-hee!

Hey! A-gonna docta come!
Bring organ-pop.
You wah-hee!

Hey! A-gonna Katie and Samuel come!
You wah-hee!

It's hard for me to talk. My thick tongue gets in the way. So the words get twisted and come out soundin' funny to some folks. When I was at the homeplace with Momma and Poppa and Katie and Samuel, Momma spoke mostly English, Poppa mostly Pennsylvania Dutch. Katie and Samuel and I spoke both. And they all could understand me.

Now I live at the County Home—the poor farm. Most folks here don't know any Dutch, and with my tongue in the way and all, who here understands what I'm tryin' to say? They call me an idiot. They say I talk gibberish. Well, Boy understands me. Boy says my poem is s'posed to sound like this:

Hey! The threshers are going to come!
Bay horse! White horse!
You watch!

Hey! The doctor is going to come!
He will bring me a mouth organ!
You watch!

Hey! Katie and Samuel are going to come!
You watch!

My poem tells three things I talk about a lot. The things I wait for.

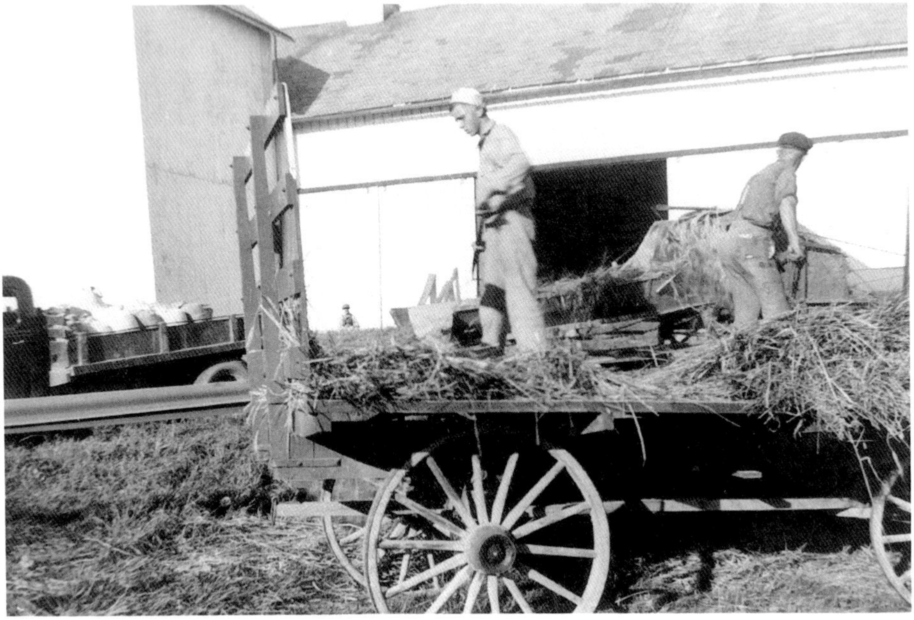

One

When I was a boy at the homeplace with Momma and Poppa and Katie and Samuel, the threshers came around every summer. They came after we'd got our wheat cut and bundled and put into shocks in the field. The threshers would drive up of an evenin', with a bay horse and a white horse a-pullin' the water wagon. Why, those horses were so big, they made our farm chunks look like ponies! Next would come another team a-pullin' the wood wagon. Then the threshin' machine itself would come steamin' into our farm lot, and the men would set it up next to where Poppa told 'em he wanted the strawstack to go. I couldn't sleep that night I was so excited!

The next mornin', men and boys from farms all around came with their teams and hayracks to help haul the bundles in from the fields. Meanwhile, the threshers were fillin' and firin' up the boiler of the steam engine and beltin' the engine to the threshin' machine. When the steam was up they blew that sad-soundin' whistle to tell everyone they were set to go. By then, the sun had burned the dew off the wheat. Then the haulers could load their wagons with the dry bundles and bring 'em back from the fields to pitch onto the feeder table of the threshin' machine.

Poppa let me sit up high in the nearby barn, by the opened doors of the hayloft, so I'd be outta harm's way but still could see all the goin's-on down below. The bundles were fed in, the grain spewed into sacks, and the straw blew out the long black spout onto our ever-growin' strawstack! The engine hissed steam! Now'n-then sparks got out, and the men watched after 'em to see they didn't land on our strawstack and catch it afire.

Now that I'm a man and live at the County Home, I still wait for the threshers to come around. But it's some different now. Every summer I look for the bay horse and the white horse to come in pullin' the water wagon. But there's no water wagon or wood wagon, and they bring no horses at all. And nowadays, no steam or sparks come outta the engine. But there is lots of noise and bustle. Bundles go in, grain comes out, and the straw is built up into a stack!

Here the farm is so big, the threshers stay three or four days to get all our wheat and oats threshed. When the day's work is done and I've had my supper, I sneak over to the threshin' place and climb up on the strawstack. Nothin's goin' on there of an evenin'. But I just set there anyway, lookin' at the machine and feelin' good till it gets dark and they come searchin' for me.

Two

Once, a long time ago, when I was a boy at the homeplace with Momma and Poppa and Katie and Samuel, Poppa brought me a mouth organ. They showed me how to blow air into it to make a nice sound. Then they showed me how to draw air out of it to make a different sound. I liked that so much, I just kept a-blowin' and a-drawin' all day long. The next day Momma started to teach me to play "Home, Sweet Home." It took quite a while, but Momma was so patient, and in a few weeks I'd learned to play the whole first line of it. That's as far as I ever got.

I carried my mouth organ with me everwhere I went. I sat on the back steps and played to the dog, but he just howled. So I went down to the barn and played for the cows at milkin' time. Poppa said it was all right, since it didn't seem to cut down any on the milk they gave. Now'n-then Katie and Samuel got a little put out with me, because when I'd finish the first line that I knew, I'd just start on blow-draw-blow-draw to finish the song. That got on their nerves. But they didn't make me stop. They could see how much

I liked playin'.

Well, I lost that mouth organ out in the garden. I'd put it in my overalls pocket when Momma sent me out to get her some tomatoes for our supper. I guess it just slipped out somewhere. I looked and looked, and Katie and Samuel helped me, but I never did find it. I felt so bad. I thought maybe Poppa would get me another one. He never did.

After I came here to the County Home, I told everyone about my mouth organ. I even told Docta once, when he came to see an old man who was sick. Docta said maybe he would bring me one, when he came the next time. But Docta didn't come very often.

One day *I* was sick, and Cook made me some ginger beer that tasted so good. It was all I could keep down for a while. Cook asked me if I wanted anything else, as she could see I felt bad. I said right off, "Organ-pop!"

She didn't understand me at first, so I held up my hands by my mouth the way I would to play, and then she understood. I got to feelin' even worse, and they called Docta to come see me.

"Docta come!" I yelled when I saw him comin' into the men's ward. He came right up to my bed and smiled at me.

"Hello, Henry, you little scamp. I hear you got yourself sick again! I see your tongue is sticking out, as usual. Now you just stick it out a little farther so I can look down your throat."

After Docta had looked at me and felt my neck and tummy, he said I had to take a spoon of medicine. But I just pushed my tongue back in and shut my mouth tight as I could, and I put my hand over my mouth. I didn't like medicine, and I warn't a-gonna take any. But I guess maybe Cook had reminded Docta what I wanted so bad—he pulled a shiny new mouth organ outta his pocket.

"Organ-pop!" I yelled. And I reached for it. Docta pulled it away and wouldn't give it to me unless I took the medicine. So I swallered it down. Then he gave me that mouth organ I'd been waitin' for and wantin' so bad for such a long time.

I got a lot better soon, and then I could blow and draw right good. I played that mouth organ all over the County Home grounds. They wouldn't let me play it inside, as some of the old folks who were stuck inside and soon to die said it made 'em feel like cryin', that "Home, Sweet Home" song. Some of 'em did cry. I didn't like to see 'em feelin' so sad, so I stayed outside to play like they'd told me to. Even there, some didn't like my playin'.

Ray said, "Can't you learn the rest of the song, you dummy? That blow-draw stuff over and over is dumb! Put your brain in a peckerwood's head, you'd starve to death in an apple orchard."

That made me feel bad. I said some words I'd learned from Poppa and Samuel that men can say when things go wrong, like when the Durham cow kicked Poppa so hard in the leg. I didn't like Ray calling me a dummy. I know Ray's smarter than me. Meaner, too.

Well, I lost that mouth organ, too. I'm not sure where. Maybe it was over by the dwindlin' strawstack where I would go sometimes to wait for the threshers to come back. The smaller that stack got, the sooner they'd be back. I know that much. Or maybe it slipped outta my pocket when I was runnin' away after I'd played a trick on Boy. I snuck up and jerked the handkerchief out of Boy's hip pocket. Then I ran away with it—I almost fell down I was chortlin' so hard. Boy ran after me and caught me round the waist, and grabbed the handkerchief back, and laughed and said, "You imp!" I liked that. I don't know what an imp is, but the way Boy said it, I know it must be good, because Boy took the joke so well and laughed so much. With all the scufflin' around over the handkerchief, I might have lost my mouth organ right then, but I was so pleased with myself I forgot to miss it till later.

Well, as soon as I found it was missin', I began to think Docta would bring me another one. I talk about it a lot. I tell everyone, "A-gonna Docta come! Bring organ-pop."

Three

Katie and Samuel come to see me now'n-then. I wait for them every Sunday afternoon. But it seems like the longer I stay here at the County Home, the less often they come. They say, "We can't come every Sunday now, Henry. There's a war on, you know. We don't get much gas."

Well, I don't know about that. I do know I miss them a lot. They're much older than me. Momma said she'd about given up on God givin' her any more children after Katie and Samuel. Then, finally, she got me. I think that made her right happy.

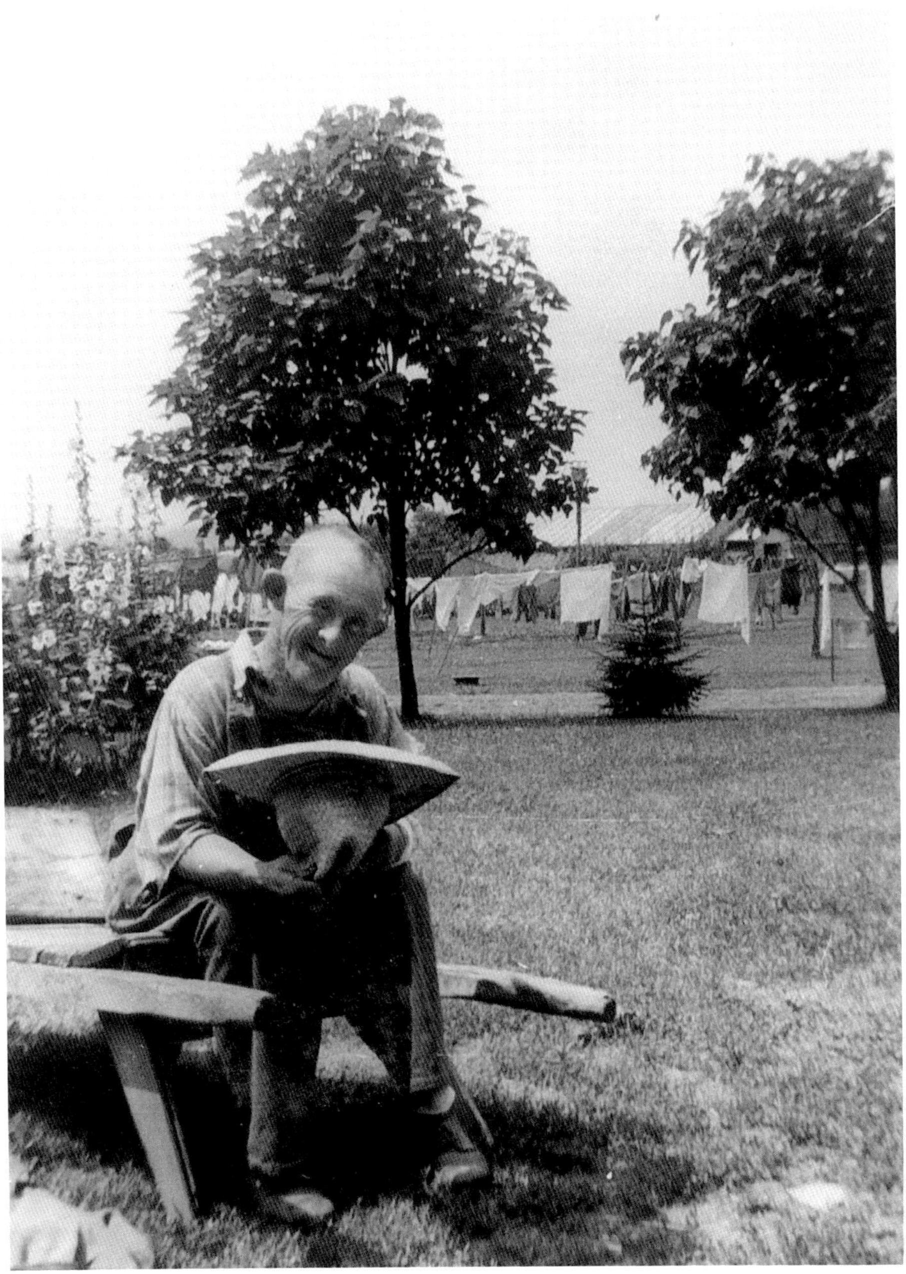

But sometimes she seemed sad about me. Like once I heard her say to Poppa, when she didn't know I was around, "What's to become of Henry when we two old gray heads are gone?"

Well, when Momma and Poppa were gone, and I finally understood it, then I found out. Katie and Samuel left me here at the County Home a long time ago, when I was scarce a man. But they said they would come to visit me, and they did. I knew they would. I'd told everyone here, "A-gonna Katie and Samuel come." I'd told everyone a lotta times.

They came one Sunday during threshin' time. We'd been threshin' here for three days, and still warn't done. Of course, that kinda work warn't done on a Sunday. After dinner at noon, I waited awhile on the bench by the garden wall. Then I thought they warn't a-gonna come, so I snuck over to the strawstack and climbed up on it. I just sat there in the warm sunshine, a-lookin' at the threshin' machine, though it was just settin' there and no one else was around. When Katie and Samuel came to the big house late that afternoon, no one could find me! They should've thought of the threshin' machine and the strawstack right off, but no one did. Not even Ray, who thinks he's so smart!

Well, finally someone remembered that's where I'd be, and they came and fetched me in. I was dirty, even though I'd had my Saturday bath. I'd torn the sleeves of my plaid shirt clear up to the shoulders and got my arms sunburned.

They took me in the back way and cleaned me up and put some salve on my arms. Then they got me another clean plaid shirt that covered up the sunburn. That shirt felt so good and smelled so nice! All the while, Katie and Samuel were waitin' for me in Boss and Missus's parlor. I s'pose they were wonderin' if the folks here had lost me clear off the poor farm.

When Missus took me into the parlor and I saw Katie and Samuel there, I got so excited! I yelled, "Katie come! Samuel come!"

I grinned a lot and chatted away. But they didn't stay long—I guess they had somewhere else to go, and it had took so long to find me and get me cleaned up. Katie stood up. She said, "We gotta go home now, Henry."

"Y'a-gonna geh heim?"

Samuel stood up too. "Yes, Henry, it's time."

Katie gave me a big hug! That felt so good, though it hurt my sunburned arms just a little. Then Samuel gave me a hug too. I hadn't had anyone to hug me for such a long time! Then they left fast. I think Katie was a-cryin'. Boss and Missus got me to go outside and I waved and waved to Katie and Samuel. I watched the dust from their wheels all the way down Infirmary Road, till they went over the rise and dropped outta sight.

After they left I felt so blue I didn't know what to do. I didn't even feel like goin' back over to see the threshin' machine. So I just sat down on the bench by the wall and ripped the sleeves of my clean shirt clear up to the shoulders.

PART THREE

TYRANNY TREMBLES: JAPAN SURRENDERS
TUESDAY, AUGUST 14, 1945

As we were finishing chores this evening, one of the old men got it over the radio and the word spread fast through the wards and the staff quarters and out to the barns. Japan has surrendered: except for the signing, the war is over!

This evening is our usual practice night for the Ridgefield Township Band. Boss had run his family's farm in that township before he became superintendent of the County Home; when he got the county job, the farm was rented out and Boss's elderly parents moved into town. Boss loves to beat the big bass drum in the band, so he still goes back to Ridgefield on practice nights to keep it up. His young daughter, Joy, is learning to play clarinet, so she has joined the band, and I play trombone.

This evening of the war's end, the three of us pile into the car as usual for the trip to Ridgefield. What is not so usual is that Ray also comes along—Ray, who can't even play a jew's-harp or a kazoo, as far as I know. We're running late, so when we get to the town, Boss lets Joy and me out right in front of the fire station, while the men drive around back to park the car. The two of us run up the outside stairs to the Grange Hall over the station, only to find the Hall's door locked and no other band members around. This has never happened before! When we get back downstairs, Boss and Ray are nowhere to be seen.

"Where are they?" I ask. "Do you think they went to your grandparents' house?"

Joy is very young, but this is her hometown and she knows the unmarked store that serves as the town's bar. So she laughs and points down the street to it. "No, Grandpa is probably down there in the bar with 'em! And they didn't come here this night to blow horns or beat drums. The war's over—don't you get it?"

Both of us are under age, so we wait for the men on a park bench under the huge elms in the town square, near the white-painted nineteenth-century bandstand. There's not another person on the square or the street; it's not much of a celebration for us. But Boss and Ray and all the men of Ridgefield Township who have gathered in that little bar tonight lift a glass together, for now they know that their sons and brothers and grandsons, all of them who are still alive, will be coming home!

All the way back from Ridgefield to the County Home, speeding down the country roads at 45, heedless of the car's tires, Boss leads the singing. We sing, "Oh! Susanna"; "I've Been Working on the Railroad"; "America, the Beautiful"; and "Columbia, the Gem of the Ocean: *Thy banners make tyranny tremble, When borne by the red, white, and blue!*"

***

I'm thinking now about Joy's question, "The war's over—don't you get it?" I don't know if I really get it. Oh, I believe it all right. It all happened so fast. Those atom bombs dropped on Japan changed everything for me. Maybe for the whole world.

The war's over, and I missed out on it. Sat it out, first in high school and then working here in this fertile, rolling, farming country, some days not thinking about the war at all.

But now I am. I'm thinking about Cousin Daniel, and the older boys from my school and neighborhood, who did get in it. I've heard of a few who got killed or wounded—lost a leg or half a face, or went crazy—or were taken prisoner or are missing in action. It ended so fast; probably there'll be more that I'll find out about in the weeks ahead. Here I am, healthy and in one piece, with no war stories to tell. Dad got his wish all right, that it would be all over before I had to go.

Maybe there won't ever be another big war. After all, we've got those atom bombs to keep a check on any country that might want to start one. That could be a good thing. Well, I'll think more about that some other time. Now I have to get to sleep, for when that five o'clock bell rings tomorrow morning, I'll need to milk some cows, war or no war.

SOUVENIRS

Early September, 1945: Boss's son, Alex, is mustered out and comes home, carrying his souvenirs from the war. When all of the staff have gathered around after supper to see them, Alex first shows us a German Luger. Then he holds up a Nazi ski trooper's fur hat.

He parts the hat's long white fur and says, "Look in here!"

We look. Buried way down deep in the fur is a tiny silver swastika. We glance around at each other and smile. The red, white, and blue has triumphed: we need not fear that swastika symbol of hate and tyranny ever again. So we think.

***

It's funny about Alex. He doesn't seem to want to tell war stories, even when I really try to pump him about the hat, how he got it.

"Did you shoot that Kraut, Alex?"

"N-n-not exactly."

"What do you mean? Did you or didn't you?"

"I shot at him. Several of us did at about the same time. One of us got him in the leg."

"Oh, so he didn't die?"

"He died."

"How, if he was just wounded in the leg?"

Alex hesitates. Finally he says, "Conditions. Conditions on the battlefield. It was war, yuh know."

That's all he'll say about it. I'm left wondering what it was really like over there. I change the subject.

"What are you going to do, Alex, now that you're getting outta the army?"

"Go back down t' Ohio State end of this month and finish Ag College. I've got just one more year t' go. After that—I don't know. Maybe go back t' farming in Ridgefield—grow things, instead of blowing 'em up. That land we've got there—it's been in our family since 1840, and I hate t' see it go inta other hands. But I'm the first in my family t' go t' college. After I get my degree I might want t' do something different. I think I'd like t' be a county agricultural agent, help other farmers. Whatever I do, I need t' stay near the land, get outside t' the fields a lot. I couldn't stand working inside in a factory, or bein' in an office all the time.

"What about you, Will?"

I like it that Alex calls me by my real name, not "Boy." I like it even more that he wants to know *my* plans.

"Well, I've gotten a lot out of my farm experience here these last five months, so I've decided to go to the Ag College down at State too, to learn more—but I don't know if I'll go into farming or the army. I'll be a freshman, so I have to go a week earlier than you, for orientation. That means I'll be leavin' here tomorrow. My dad's comin' with his car to fetch me back home, so I can get ready and pack up my school clothes and things. Then I'll be takin' the train from Cleveland to Columbus. Maybe I'll see yuh there on campus sometime?"

"Probably will, Will." Alex laughs at the two "wills" he's just said, and goes on, "I'll be catchin' the Greyhound down at the other end of Infirmary Road, at the paved highway, unless I can find a good used car t' buy before I leave. I want t' get my own car soon as I can. It'll be easier t' get home. Yuh know, after bein' away so long, I need t' get back here quite a few weekends t' get reacquainted with my family. Joy was just a little girl when I left; now she's almost a teen-ager!

"Maybe you could come along some weekend too?"

"I'd like that, Alex. I think I'm gonna miss this place, and all the folks here."

***

I wander outside to take a last look around. Many of the old men are sitting out on the benches in the yard, having their last pipes of the evening. I shake hands, tell them I'll be leaving in the morning, that I was glad to have known them. I walk slowly past the well, the garden, the corn crib, milk house, dairy barn, and across and along Infirmary Road from the potter's field past the toolshed and the other barn to the near pasture. The dairy cows have been turned out there for the night. I take a last long look at the two Holsteins and the smaller red cow I have milked twice a day for the past five months. Then

I look over at the big house across the road, trying to fix it in my mind. In the growing darkness, as I stroll along between the pasture fence and the county drainage ditch that parallels the road, a muskrat slips into the water with a very soft *blip-ip.* I *know* I'm going to miss this place.

I see Ray striding toward me. As I cross over the ditch to meet him he says, "I jest wanted t' say goodbye t' yuh now, away from the others. I own up t' it, when I first set eyes on yuh I didn't think yuh could do the job here. Oh, yuh messed up a few times, but yuh larned a lot and got the work done. Lookatchuh!—I bet yuh've growed an inch and put on twenty pounds of muscle since yuh come here last spring. Yuh've growed from a boy to a young man!

"Best a luck t' yuh, Will."

"Thanks, Ray."

I want to say more, but Ray has already wheeled around and is re-crossing Infirmary Road, walking swiftly back toward the big house, leaving me the best souvenir a boy, or a young man, could ever want. He called me... *Will!*

AFTERWORD

Brief History of County Poor Farms and Their Successors

County poor farms were facilities in a rural setting that provided housing and care for needy residents of a county. These facilities, also known as poor farms, poorhouses, or workhouses, and often later as county infirmaries and finally as county homes, were common in the United States from the mid-1800s through the early 1950s. They were publicly funded and maintained by county taxes and/or bond issues, as contrasted with church and other private charitable sources that operate soup kitchens and provide temporary or permanent shelter to the homeless.

On these county farms able-bodied residents would work to produce crops or commodities such as milk, butter, meat, and eggs in exchange for meals and shelter. The food produced was used to feed the residents or was sold to help support the farm. Those who were unable to work in the fields handled cooking, cleaning, and upkeep of the main house, or helped care for other residents or performed light chores about the grounds. Some few who chose to live in the county home and who could pay for their upkeep were not required to work but could if they wished to.

The residents were almost always referred to, without apology, as inmates, a term that may offend our politically correct notions of today. But that was yesterday. They were the elderly, the sick, orphaned or abandoned of all ages, as well as the physically or emotionally disabled. Thrown together, they struggled with life out of the way of most of society, usually until they ended up in the facility's potter's field for burial after their death.

In time, state laws required the removal of most of the children to separate living arrangements.

Populations at these facilities boomed during the Great Depression of the 1930s. Yet, government programs of the Depression, such as public works programs and the beginning of payouts after the Social Security Act of 1935 was passed, contributed to a decline in the number of county farms.

Many of the facilities lingered on as infirmaries, nursing homes, and sometimes orphanages, but for the most part, the working farm that had brought its disparate residents together began to disappear. The farm acreage might be sold off or leased to local farmers or converted to use by other county agencies. The potter's field, entirely forgotten or perhaps remembered by only a small historical marker, might be plowed and planted to crops, or paved over for a parking lot, or overgrown with weeds, or planted to grass for a playground.

The main buildings of these farms met various fates over the years. Some were sold to private owners, Others were torn down, and still others were allowed to sit unused. Some are on historical registers and remain publicly owned. At least one survives as a county home museum. In rare instances the main building continued as a publicly supported and operated home, but with many more paying residents than in earlier days, and no longer associated with a working farm.

The roads that led to county poor farms, named Poor Farm Road, County Farm Road, County Home Road, or Infirmary Road, sometimes retained their names, but in other instances they were renamed to no longer indicate the connection to the facility they had served for so many years.

Some sources of the above information, in addition to personal observations and memories of the author are:

1. Wikipedia
2. http://www.poorhousestory.com
3. Minnesota Public Radio's excellent feature, Over the Hill to the Poorhouse, July 29, 2002, by Dan Gunderson and Chris Julin. Much of this feature can be reached through Source 2, above.